IN SUNSHINE BRIGHT

and

DARKNESS DEEP

READ ORDER

26	141 (14)	37	154
67		52	187
130		9	208
175 (12)		79	
		97	
		114	

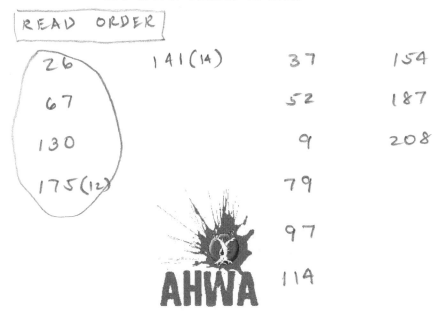

AHWA

An Anthology of Australian Horror

In Sunshine Bright and Darkness Deep
Published by the Australian Horror Writers' Association
Edited by Cameron Trost, Ben Knight, and the AHWA committee
Cover art and design by Greg Chapman
Copyright © AHWA, 2015
www.australianhorror.com

The River Slurry © Rue Karney
Triage © Jason Nahrung
Upon the Dead Oceans © Marty Young
Beast © Natalie Satakovski
The Grinning Tide © Stuart Olver
Our Last Meal © J. Ashley Smith
Veronica's Dogs © Cameron Trost
Bullets © Joanne Anderton
Saviour © Mark McAuliffe
The Hunt © Mark Smith-Briggs
The Monster in the Woods © Kathryn Hore
Road Trip © Anthony Ferguson
Bloodlust © Steve Cameron
Elffingern © Dan Rabarts

Triage by Jason Nahrung was first printed in EnVision
Fantastic Visions Media, 2005

National Library of Australia Cataloguing-in-Publication entry

Title: In sunshine bright and darkness deep: an anthology of Australian horror / [edited by Cameron Trost and the AHWA committee ; Greg Chapman, cover artist]

Subjects: Horror tales, Australian.

A823.087

ISBN: 978-1508670384

To the scribes of the Australian Horror Writers' Association.
May the sunshine bright and darkness deep of our vast and
mysterious land always inspire you.

The Australian Horror Writers' Association (AHWA) is a non-profit organisation that was founded unofficially in 2003 as a way of providing a unified voice and a sense of community for Australian writers of dark fiction, while helping the development and evolution of this genre within Australia. This anthology, the first of its kind to be published by the AHWA, is a showcase of work contributed by several of our active members. For more information about us, our members, or to join, visit the website at:

www.australianhorror.com

Introduction

In Sunshine Bright and Darkness Deep is an anthology like no other. The tales herein will take you on a weird and terrifying journey. You will set out on a road trip and find yourself trapped in the arid Australian outback where a little girl and her grandfather struggle to survive. There are isolated farmhouses threatened by bushfires and bullets, and rainforests teeming with bloodthirsty bugs. The cities are full of trouble too. The murky waters of the Brisbane River hide spiteful spirits and the suburbs are infested with insane inhabitants masquerading as ordinary human beings. Then, you will leave Australia, departing from Melbourne, to hunt down vampiric gangsters in Southeast Asia, before sailing future seas and visiting realms beyond this world altogether.

This inaugural showcase anthology features the work of just a handful of the many talented and darkly imaginative authors who make up the Australian Horror Writers' Association. If you are unfamiliar with Australian horror, let this book be just the first step on a long voyage of discovery.

On behalf of our members, we thank you for your support and trust you will enjoy these tales of horror.

When you are ready, lock the doors, bolt the windows, and turn the page.

- AHWA Committee, January 2015

THE RIVER SLURRY
Rue Karney

'How did you sustain your injury, Mr Waldram?' Dr Gadot sat at her desk, her pen poised above a sheet of paper.

'I wanted to finish off a few things around the house before the baby arrived. I was putting wood through a plane. Next thing I know, I'm in hospital minus four fingers.'

'You were distracted? Lost concentration?'

'Not really,' Kurt Waldram replied, tapping his foot on the carpeted floor. 'Rushing things, probably. You know how it is, too much to do and never enough time.'

'Is your work stressful?'

'It can be. I'm a writer and researcher on the show, *Lore, Legends and Lies*, so a lot of working to tight deadlines.' He smiled. 'Are you a fan?'

'Of what? Tight deadlines?'

'No.' Kurt's foot tapped faster. 'Of the TV show.'

'I don't watch commercial television.' Dr Gadot scribbled as she spoke. 'You're finding the prosthetic fingers suitable for your work?'

'I can type.' Kurt gave a half laugh. 'But mostly I use voice recognition software.'

'And why is that?' She held the pen above the sheet of paper again, and shifted forward in her chair. Her hazel eyes fixed on the four artificial digits on Kurt's left hand.

'Voice recognition is easier, I suppose.' He shrugged. 'The prosthetics feel…weird.'

Dr Gadot moved around to Kurt's side of the desk. She picked up his left hand and massaged the muscles and tendons below his knuckles. As she pressed and kneaded, the itch started.

'You find them hard to control?' She pressed her index finger hard against each of his metacarpophalangeal joints.

'No, they work okay.'

He gritted his teeth as the doctor prodded and pressed up his flesh and bone stump to the start of his plastic prosthetic. The itch started to burn.

'Pain?'

An invisible hot knife sliced across the space Kurt's missing fingers used to inhabit. The edge of his lips twisted in a grimace.

'If it's hurting too much, just tell me.' Her fingers probed up and down his prosthetics.

Kurt knew he should not feel any sensation in his absent fingers. It was impossible, he told himself, to feel a maddening itch or stab of hot pain in an empty, finger-sized space, but as Dr Gadot pressed and squeezed, pain drummed through his inexistent flesh and bone.

His stomach squirmed. His head spun. Sweat trickled from his hairline, down his temples.

Dr Gadot let his hand go and handed him a box of tissues.

'Sorry.' He pressed a tissue against his mouth and slumped in his chair.

'It's a common reaction.' She sat back behind her desk and scribbled more notes onto her writing pad.

'Reaction to what?'

'Phantom pain.' She put down her pen. 'However, phantom is somewhat of a misnomer. Your pain exists, Mr Waldram. There is no doubt about that.'

'So I'm stuck with it.'

'Not at all. You're an excellent candidate for mirror box therapy. Every individual responds differently, of course, but with regular sessions using the mirror box, I expect you will be pain free in less than two months.'

A bolt of pain shot through each of Kurt's missing fingers. 'When can we start?'

#

Silvie jabbed at the whiteboard with the tip of her fake fingernail. 'Kurt, the River Slurry. Progress report?'

'Yeah, it's going well.'

Silvie opened her palms, signalling *and?*

'I'm chasing up some leads from 1973—'

'Eyewitnesses from the 2011 floods?'

He jiggled his knee under the desk. 'Still working on that.'

Silvie's narrow nostrils flared. Around the room, the rest of the *Lore, Legends and Lies* team focused their eyes anywhere but on Silvie or Kurt.

'Find people.' She punctuated each word with a point of her finger. 'Make them talk to you.'

Kurt suspected Silvie knew there wasn't enough material behind the River Slurry story to make a solid piece. She'd made it clear she wanted him gone, and up until this assignment, every time she'd tried to prove him incompetent, he'd managed to triumph. But the River Slurry had him stumped.

He stared out the window at the dirty brown Brisbane River. A blue-trimmed ferry cut diagonally across the water, leaving a muddy wake fringed with yellow scum. A single figure leaned over the edge of the ferry's safety rail and threw something into the water. The object bobbed and glittered on the river's oily surface for a moment. The wake snatched at it, dragged it into its scum and sucked it under, into the brown deep.

I'll give her a River Slurry story, Kurt's plastic prosthetics tapped on his tablet, that'll grip her by her scrawny neck and shake her until she throws up.

#

'How have your pain levels been this week?' Dr Gadot gestured for Kurt to sit down on the two-seater sofa in the corner of her office.

'A little better.'

'Are you sleeping well?'

'Okay, I suppose.' Kurt gave a wry grin. 'Between the pain and the baby, sleep loses out.'

'And work?'

'Fine.' His foot tapped a triple beat against the carpet. 'Work's okay.'

'Well then. Let's begin.' Dr Gadot reached under the table and pulled out the square mirror, unfolded the pieces of cardboard beneath it and sat it on the table between them.

12

Kurt put his good hand next to the mirror and lay his injured hand flat inside the triangular box. 'Same as last time?'

'Yes.' Dr Gadot nodded. 'Just like piano scales. Focus on the image in the mirror and let your injured hand relax.' She glanced at his feet. 'Relax your whole body.'

Kurt breathed out. He stared into the mirror and pressed his fingertips against it one by one until they all touched its surface. He repeated the movement, gritting his teeth against the needles of pain shooting through the not-there fingers attached to his hand inside the box.

'Eyes on the mirror, Kurt. Keep your movements even. Work through the pain.'

Kurt spidered his fingertips against the mirror over and over again, performing the movement to a bass riff inside his head until Dr Gadot's voice became a distant whisper. His world shrunk to his hand and the mirror and the bass riff until he was no longer in a doctor's office but inside a space in the mirror. Here, another version of himself existed, a version with all fingers and zero pain. His fingers slid against one another, fingertip to fingertip, nail to nail.

'Good work today, Kurt.' Dr Gadot's voice snapped him out of his inner world.

Kurt flexed his finger stubs. 'The pain is a lot better.'

'You've made excellent progress.' She gestured toward the mirror box. 'Increase your practice at home to two sessions of one hour per day. I will see you in a fortnight.'

#

The shadow in the mirror didn't appear until Kurt's third week of therapy. He had been diligent, working his fingers with the mirror box an hour before work and an hour after dinner. Naomi never complained.

'Spend as much time as you need,' Naomi reassured him, putting a grizzling Lucas on her shoulder and patting his back to encourage a burp. 'You're no help when you're in pain. With any luck, this treatment will have you a hundred per cent before he starts teething.'

Kurt practised in the study, with the mirror box on his desk, closing the door to avoid distractions. He worked methodically through the program Dr Gadot had set, his fingers playing the mirrored surface like piano scales.

When he first saw the shadow, he thought it was a smudge. He grabbed a tissue and rubbed it against the mirror. When that didn't shift the mark, he shone the desk lamp onto its surface. The shadow disappeared. He continued his exercises and forgot about it until the end of the hour when he got up and turned off the lights.

A flicker caught his eye. He squinted into the gloom, then switched the light on again and checked the box's mirrored surface. There was nothing.

He shut the study door behind him, and went into the nursery to check on Lucas. The baby's small red lips were parted in a pout, and breath whistled in and out of his tiny nose.

Nine weeks old. So small.

Kurt brushed his fingertips across the top of the thatch of fine dark hair that covered his son's scalp. His fingers rested for a moment on the fontanelle; the soft membrane pulsed beneath his touch.

So fragile.

He pressed his lips gently against his sleeping son's cheek and listened to his soft, whistling snore.

'Sleep tight, my little man.'

A wave of anxiety washed around Kurt's stomach. He turned, checked left and right. He opened the cupboard doors and peered inside. He pulled the curtain back, then let it fall. He stood and listened, but the only sound was his son's breathing. As he left the room, he checked once more, corner to corner. He didn't see anything in the shadows.

#

Kurt pressed his palms against the pain that thumped behind his temples. Another eight hours of combing through archived videos, photographs, text and audio had brought him no closer to the elusive River Slurry. He'd found a couple of newspaper stories about a female mud monster dating back to the 1893 floods, a dozen or so letters to the editor and a couple more stories from the 1973 floods that mentioned the same mysterious female figure lurking in shadows, leaving slicks of mud-like slime on scrubbed and polished floors. He'd traced the first use of the River Slurry name to a tabloid headline from 1973, and tracked down the journalist whose byline appeared with the article.

'A bit of gory entertainment to mesmerise the masses, mate. Nothing more.' The old guy sipped at his beer as they looked out across the brown expanse of murky river. 'The River Slurry is about as real as my left eye.' He pulled out his glass orb and popped it on the table. It rolled across the plastic, and rested against a bottle cap.

'What about the slicks of mud left on clean floors?' Kurt kept his gaze fixed on the river. 'And the missing babies?'

'Mud is mud.' The old journo sighed. 'But those little babies. Turned out it was some poor girl who'd had her own baby taken away from her. Sent her mad, she kept looking for it, going into people's homes and taking babies from their cots. Took the cops a couple of months to sort that mess out. Last I heard, they locked her up in Wolston Park Asylum.' He sipped his beer and shook his head. 'Poor girl. She's probably dead now.'

Kurt tapped his foot against the verandah floorboards. 'I had an old auntie in that place.'

'In Wolston Park?' The journo grimaced. 'Poor thing. You're ever looking for a horror story, just spend a night there. There's laws against what used to pass as treatments in that hell-hole.'

The three reported stories from 2011 had been proven fakes. One of them an excellent fake, which is why the urban legend still hung around, giving Sylvie a legitimate reason for making it into a giant pain in Kurt's arse. He was determined to beat her at her petty game; to find that something that would have believers shuddering and set sceptics scrambling. He gritted his teeth against the thumping behind his temples and ran the excellent fake video again, searching for that tiny detail that could help him conjure irrefutable evidence from vague conjecture. He studied it frame by frame, his eyes dry and stinging, until the throbbing in his head shifted to the spaces where his fingers used to be.

The pain stabbed like a hot dagger. He stopped the video and took his mirror box from the bottom drawer of his desk. He set it up and laid his injured hand inside the box, and began the familiar piano scale exercise, spidering his whole fingers up and down the mirror in time to the bass riff inside his head. His world shrank down to a pinpoint. The pulses of pain faded and the riff shifted to a soothing lullaby.

'Hush, little Lukie, don't say a word,' he sang along to the tune inside his head, 'daddy's going to buy you a mockingbird.'

Lucas loved the lullaby, he settled each time Kurt sang it to him.

'And if that mockingbird don't sing, daddy's going to buy you a diamond ring.'

As Kurt exercised his fingers, the familiar female-shaped shadow formed on the mirror's surface. Over the past few sessions, the shadow had become a comfort to him, because as the shadow deepened, his pain vanished.

'And if that diamond ring turns brass, daddy's going to buy you a looking glass.'

A flicker of movement from the screen caught his eye. He pressed play and switched between watching the video frames flick past, second by second, and watching the shadow in the mirror.

Kurt hit pause. In the video frame, a muddy female shape stained the blue sky background. The flesh on his forearms prickled as he glanced back and forth, mirror to frame, frame to mirror, and identical facial features morphed and sharpened from mirror surface to screen.

'Looking glass...looking glass...' A female voice trilled inside Kurt's head.

Kurt jumped up. His chair clattered against the white tiled floor. He sucked in a breath, then forced it out slow and steady through his mouth. He leaned forward, hands on the edge of his desk, and checked the mirror.

His own brown eyes stared back at him. The white of his left eye had a distinct red vein shaped like a crooked smile.

Kurt's missing fingers tingled. He turned away from the mirror, moving his finger stubs toward the video frame frozen on the screen. The tingle intensified into an itch.

The face in the video frame blinked, and in its muddy eye, a small red vein cracked its own crooked smile.

Kurt's heart thumped in his chest.

The figure in the video thickened and swelled, and reached its arm, hand and fingers out of the screen toward him.

A chill shook Kurt's body, head to toe. He shut his eyes, forced himself to breathe in until his belly swelled, then breathe out again.

When he opened his eyes, the frozen video frame was filled with blue sky and brown river, and nothing else.

Kurt turned the monitor off. He snatched his mirror box and hurried out of the office.

\#

'You seem stressed.' Dr Gadot touched Kurt lightly on his elbow and ushered him into her office. 'Is everything okay?'

'No... I mean, yes.' Kurt frowned and rubbed his fingers across his temples. 'Everything's fine. It's just work stuff.'

'Give me your hand.' She massaged the muscles and tendons below his knuckle stubs. 'Are you finding the prosthetics easier to use?'

'Yes.' Kurt twisted his lips.

'Pain?'

'No, it's not...' Kurt barked a laugh. 'It's stupid but...' He hesitated. 'Have any of your other patients reported seeing something in the mirror, something that's not, that shouldn't be... there.'

'Something like?' She sat back and took her notepad.

'A shadow... or a figure...'

A faint crease furrowed Dr Gadot's brow.

Kurt scratched his head. 'I'm sorry, I'm being stupid. Researching urban myths and legends makes me overthink things sometimes.'

Dr Gadot gave a tight smile. 'Perhaps you're working a bit too hard, Mr Waldram. You are looking quite fatigued.'

'Twelve-hour work days and up half the night with the baby.' His foot tapped a fast beat on the carpet.

'Any other symptoms concerning you?' She tapped her pen on her notepad. 'Any other visual disturbances? Hearing voices—'

'No, no, it's nothing like that.'

'If you're concerned, I can refer you to a psychiatrist.'

Sure, and they'll send me the same way as my poor old

auntie.

'Pardon?' Dr Gadot frowned.

'No, really. Like I said, between work stuff and a new baby, I'm not getting much sleep.' Kurt pressed his good hand against his knee to stop it from jiggling. 'That's all it is.'

'Okay.' Dr Gadot glanced over her shoulder. She pressed her lips into a thin line as she added to her notes. 'Continue with the mirror box therapy, but if you have any concerns, any at all, call my office.'

'Sure.' Kurt smiled, and ignored the muddy woman standing behind Dr Gadot's chair, staring at him with his own eyes.

#

'What's this crap?' Silvie threw the script down on Kurt's desk.

Kurt's shoulders tensed. Needles of pain shot down his arm and into his missing fingers. He flexed his prosthetics and drew in a deep breath.

'It's the River Slurry story.' He swivelled around in his chair and faced Silvie. 'A genuine female mud monster borne out of river floods who steals babies and leaves nothing behind but a slick of mud.'

'This is all you could come up with?' Silvie's nostrils flared. 'Three pages, Kurt. Three flimsy, badly researched pages.'

'Come off it.' Kurt snorted. 'Compared to the story you ran on the woman who had spider eggs growing in her eye, this

20

story is rock solid.'

'That story was based on fact. Our main witness, if you recall, was a respected optometrist.'

'She was one of your drinking buddies, and you owed her a spot on the show after losing a bet.'

'Irrelevant!' Silvie snapped. 'She presented as a highly credible witness and the story rated through the roof. This,' she jabbed her finger at the script, 'is about as convincing as a beardless Santa.'

Kurt rolled his eyes. In his peripheral vision, he caught a glimpse of the River Slurry peering out from his screen.

Show yourself, bitch!

'What?' Silvie's voice increased in pitch from screech to banshee. 'What did you call me?'

'Nothing.' A pit of dread opened up in Kurt's guts.

Did I really say that out loud?

'What are you mumbling about?'

A bolt of pain shot through Kurt's absent fingers. He reached into his bottom drawer and grabbed his mirror box. He set it up on his desk and shoved his injured hand inside.

'What the hell are you doing now?'

'Dealing with my pain.' Kurt scaled his whole fingers up and down the mirror as the River Slurry slid from screen to mirror to behind Silvie and around again, leaving a thin slick of grey-brown mud in her wake.

'Put that stupid contraption away and get to work.' Silvie grabbed at the mirror box. The River Slurry clamped herself behind Kurt's back and pushed Silvie away.

Silvie stumbled. 'You arsehole!' She screwed up her face.

'What's that stench? Ugh!' She sniffed and clamped her hand over her mouth as she backed away toward the window. 'Have you… soiled yourself?'

'Don't be stupid.' The River Slurry's dank stench filled Kurt's nostrils. 'It's the river.'

'The river?' Silvie slammed her open palm against the window. 'The river is down there, Kurt. Behind glass. Behind the expressway.' She slammed her palm again. 'We cannot smell the river up here.'

Her words echoed around the silent office. Kurt lowered his eyes to the floor and followed the trail of muddy footprints from his desk to the window. The River Slurry's shadowy figure stained grey-brown against the blue sky. Her mouth peeled open in a leering grin.

'You've got 'til ten o'clock tomorrow morning to fix that script!' Silvie thumped her palm against the window again. 'Fix it or you're fired.' She pulled her hand away from the window and stared at the grey shadow staining her hand as Kurt walked away.

#

Naomi pushed the study door open, and Lucas' screams filled the room.

'You have to take him.' Naomi sagged against the door frame. 'Take him out in the car, in the pram. Just take him.' She burst into tears.

The hairs on the back of Kurt's neck stiffened. The River Slurry's dank stench of stagnant mud wafted from the paused video frame on his screen.

'Ten more minutes, Naomi. I'm almost done.'

'You said that two hours ago.' Naomi sobbed. 'Please Kurt, I can't... I can't...'

'Fine.' He stood and pushed the chair behind him; it skittered on its rollers and hit the desk with a thump that sent Lucas' cries up another ten decibels. 'Come here, little man.' He took Lucas from his wife's arms.

She stepped back, and a flicker of doubt crossed her red-rimmed eyes.

'Go to bed. I'll look after him.' Kurt pushed his elbow out toward Naomi, nudging her into the hall. He shut the study door, and snibbed the lock.

'Hush, hush.' Kurt rocked his baby in his arms. 'Hush, little baby.'

A shiver rippled across Kurt's back. The putrid stink of stagnant mud, effluence, and countless scraps of flood-borne flotsam and jetsam hung in the air.

Kurt breathed it in, and the stench filled his lungs.

'Hush, little baby, don't say a word, daddy's gonna buy you a mockingbird.'

He faced the screen, rocking Lucas in his arms.

'And if that mockingbird don't sing, daddy's gonna buy you a diamond ring.'

The River Slurry's shadow pulsed in the paused video. Kurt swung his baby to and fro, watching as the shadow figure slid from the screen and poured onto the faded crimson rug on the office floor.

'And if that diamond ring turns brass, daddy's gonna buy

you a looking glass.'

The shadow stained the rug an oily grey-brown. The table lamp glowed dully across the stain, and the heat of its light revealed a wrinkled scummy skin. Small brown bubbles collided together, doubling and tripling and quadrupling like cells, and the stain bubbled and popped and gathered itself together into a shape.

'And if that looking glass gets broke, daddy's gonna get you a river-mud ghost.'

The mud slick surged and stretched, and the stench of foetid mud filled the room. Kurt held Lucas tight against his chest, humming the lullaby, and the baby's cries quietened into sobs, then hiccups, as Kurt watched the River Slurry rise from the swampy pool, the mud taking shape into her legs, her torso, her neck and arms and head.

Kurt looked into the eyes of the River Slurry, and saw his own eyes looking back at him.

The River Slurry held her arms out, and Kurt saw his own arms being held out toward him. The River Slurry stretched her hands and fingers out, and Kurt saw they were his hands, his fingers, all ten of them, whole and strong.

His left hand tingled and itched, and a bolt of pain shot up from his knuckles and stabbed through his missing fingers. The pain throbbed and burned in the empty spaces where his fingers once were. Kurt pressed Lucas against his chest, struggling to hold him as he doubled over.

The sewer stench of the River Slurry coated Kurt's nostrils and throat as she shuffled toward him with outstretched arms, hands, and fingers.

Lucas arched his back and screamed.

The pain in Kurt's absent fingers squeezed and crushed his missing bones. He stared into the River Slurry's face, his face.

'Kurt, let me in!' Naomi's fists pounded on the locked door.

Kurt gazed into his mud-brown eyes, and his heart squelched and sucked as one with the River Slurry's.

'Kurt!' Naomi's body thumped against the door.

Lucas stiffened his legs. His small red face wouldn't stop screaming.

'Kurt! Open the door!' A hard object smashed against it, splintering the wood.

A gush of air sucked at Kurt's eardrums. His ears emptied of sound, then filled with the roar of rushing water. The chill of deep mud slicked up his fingers and hands, numbing them, as Lucas rolled into the arms of the River Slurry.

The door gave way. Naomi rushed into the room.

Kurt looked down at his muddy hands with their ten intact fingers. They were empty.

He did not hear Naomi scream.

TRIAGE
Jason Nahrung
For Andy

Nosplentyn hunched further into his coat as he approached the hospital entrance. The cloying scent of antiseptic washed over him. He pulled his hood tighter and wished he could dampen his enhanced senses. Nose twitching, eyes squinting, he took shallow breaths through his mouth as he entered the brightly lit foyer.

Sorrow oozed from this place. The grief penetrated his psychic defences like the air conditioning seeping through his coat. No amount of antiseptic could cleanse the reek of despair.

He wasn't helping. Most came here hoping to get better; he had come to kill.

A brain tweak got him past the guards manning the metal detector and x-ray machine. He was in no mood to answer annoying questions about what he was doing here at two in the morning.

The Council had given him this assignment, as much a test of his continuing loyalty as an acknowledgement of the detective skills he'd acquired in his former life. He'd never expected his training would one day be used for assassination. The Council didn't like trespassers poaching their food supply, any more than they tolerated disobedience.

Nosplentyn headed for the lift.

He waited with his back to a wall and wished he had worn

his robe. A legacy from the master who'd trained him; he found it a comfort, a way of marking his removal from the world he had known. Nosplentyn had thought it would have been too conspicuous for this mission, but in retrospect, he supposed the image of a monk walking the halls of a hospital might not be so out of place. But if someone looked under his hood, they would not believe he should be walking around at all.

Ping!

He jumped, though the lift's bell sounded muted in the early morning stillness. Embarrassed by his nervous reaction, he quickly stepped in and punched the button for the fourth floor.

This was his third night staking out the hospital, and hopefully the last. The sorrow was getting harder to purge.

Admittedly, there were flashes of hope, and great love too. The nurses exuded compassion, though some burned more brightly than others. At the end of the day, though, they were just delaying the inevitable, curing one ill so another could take its place, even if it was just old age. It was no different inside the hospital than out, really; just the people outside weren't so aware of their condition. They used different forms of pain management — booze, shopping, sex, television — but deep down, they knew they all shared the same prognosis.

Not his problem, not anymore. Not since he'd been turned. If he could go back to that moment, with the choice between a painful death or this immortality, which option would he take? Neither held much appeal compared to option C — be a father, be a husband. Be a good cop with enough sense not to stick his nose into the wrong conspiracy.

Nosplentyn felt the world around him growing thin and quickly reined in his regrets. Spirits pulled back into their own realm, taunted by his proximity, frustrated by his withdrawal.

'Get a grip,' Nosplentyn whispered as he crept down an empty corridor to ward 4C. This was where the worst of the worst came for their chemo. The spirit plane loomed close here, lurking behind the framed prints decorating the scuffed, off-white walls. Nosplentyn didn't look at the pictures too closely. Not even the alluring aroma of blood bags could dismiss the unnerving sensation of being watched from behind the landscapes.

A sign at the entrance told visitors to wash their hands and ensure mobile phones were turned off. Nosplentyn couldn't prevent feeling a twinge of hypocrisy as he rubbed the sweet-smelling soap into the scarred skin of his hands. As if having clean hands would make any difference when he'd found his quarry.

The sole nurse at the duty station was working her second shift in a row. Her tired mind readily accepted Nosplentyn's mental suggestion to ignore him as he stalked to the door of room eight and glanced through. No one there but the sleeping patient, his name written in marking pen on a tag above his bed, easy to read in the room's ambient light.

Nosplentyn slipped inside.

The patient already bore the mark. The wound had been supernaturally healed, but Nosplentyn could see its afterimage, there on the inside of his arm. The rogue vampire had taken blood straight from the vein, rather than pollute the taste by withdrawing from the Hickman's line permanently inserted in the man's chest.

'How are you feeling tonight, Mr Smith?' Nosplentyn whispered, running a quick eye over the blood results pinned to a clip board. 'Still mortal, I see.'

The patient had received blood earlier; Nosplentyn could smell it, see it in the patient's re-invigorated complexion. Now a bag of Lasix dripped from the IV stand along with another of antibiotics, both pumping through the multiple mouths of the Hickman's. The patient had a catheter, too, to catch the results of the Lasix once the fluid started running. The thought of having a tube inserted in his prick made Nosplentyn squirm, though he'd left such mundane concerns behind him.

Photos on the corkboard near the bed made a welcome distraction. Some new ones had been added since Nosplentyn's visit the previous night. Two little girls; one dressed like a fairy, the other with her face painted as a butterfly. Mr Smith's daughters, Nosplentyn presumed. Too young to draw more than stick figures and swirling lines of crayon, but old enough to know which blobs were daddy and mummy.

Nosplentyn turned away from the pictures, wondering if his own child had learned to draw any better. How old? Three, now? That made it four years since he had stumbled into the vampire world and, unwittingly, been made a part of it. His wife had been pregnant when he'd died. He hoped she told their daughter about him, but he knew it wouldn't be enough. How could the child remember a father she had never known?

He had been allowed to see his daughter once, the better to

know what he risked should he fail to follow orders. He swore that situation would change, but for now, he had no choice but to obey.

Nosplentyn watched the young man breathing unevenly in his morphine sleep. His maroon and gold beanie had slipped to the side, revealing a pale, unnaturally bald scalp. Not even the recent infusion of platelets could disguise the sunken cheeks, the hollow eyes, the thin lips. Muscles sagged like molten plastic. Death was close, a shadow reaching through from the other side.

In a moment of self-pity, Nosplentyn felt jealous. That release from fear, from responsibility… from the weight of the great game where the rules were totally biased against the players. But he looked again at the drawings and photographs, and knew that the burden of duty was welcomed. Pain was the price of joy and this man had paid it willingly.

Nosplentyn dodged a clump of limp helium balloons that proclaimed a recent birthday as he pulled a chair into the darkest corner. A teddy bear with a red bow stared silently from the window sill, surrounded by get well cards. Like throwing paper planes at a cyclone, but it was important for the patient to know he wasn't facing the storm alone. Loneliness could kill as sure as cancer.

Sitting huddled in the corner, Nosplentyn tried to draw comfort as he pulled shadows around himself. He hoped the rogue would come tonight. Not only was he tired of this place, but the Council was getting frustrated at the lack of progress. A source of food as rich as the hospital could not be compromised.

Finally, he heard the sound of the ward nurse approaching. A different one to last night. Please, let it be her...

She was a pretty girl, appearing too finely boned for hefting the handicapped bodies of adults around beds and showers. Red curls framed her peaches-and-cream complexion. She smelled of lilies; lilies and blood.

Nosplentyn tensed.

The nurse leaned over the man in the bed and caressed his sallow cheek.

'I'm so sorry,' she whispered, 'but it's the best I can offer. You will live on, for ever, in me.' She touched her breast, so pert under her crisp white uniform.

Her fangs slid out as she tilted the man's head to one side. His carotid bobbed weakly and he mumbled in his sleep.

'How can you stand the taste of his blood?' Nosplentyn asked.

Startled, she sprang back. The patient's head lolled. His eyes flickered but couldn't resist the combined pull of morphine and exhaustion.

'Who the fuck are you?' the nurse asked, crouching behind the bed, her gaze flicking between Nosplentyn and the door.

'I've been sent to have a word. A final word.'

She straightened.

'I see.' She looked down at the patient as Nosplentyn stepped forward into the room's subdued light, allowing his shadows to fall away.

He really would have preferred to have been wearing his robe. Somehow, it would have felt more official than army boots, cargo pants, and hoodie.

'He's dying, you know,' the nurse said, and caressed the man's forehead as Nosplentyn stopped at the foot of the bed. Her hand shook.

Nosplentyn nodded. 'They all are.'

'He's a good father, a gifted musician.' She fondled a silver ankh on a chain around her throat. 'Why should that be lost through no fault of his own?'

'That's life,' Nosplentyn snarled, gesturing with a clawed hand, fangs extending. The memory hit him with a sudden rush that made him gasp: the ambush, the flames, the pain, and the stranger leaning over him, refusing to let him pass through to the peace that waited so near he could almost reach out and touch it…

The nurse ran.

Nosplentyn cursed his momentary distraction and gave chase.

Damn, this place is getting to me, all right.

He caught her in the hallway, pushed her against a wall so hard a print fell. Glass shattered across the polished floor.

His claw drew blood from her throat as he pinned her. The wall flexed, suddenly elastic as the spirit world reacted to her fear, his frustration. Nosplentyn paused, fighting to seal the rift. It did not help that the nurse, aware of his hesitation, if not the cause, was trying to mentally manipulate his psyche as well.

'His youngest daughter just turned two,' the nurse said, voice pleading, eyes wide and shining with tears. 'She'll barely remember him at all.'

Nosplentyn's grip loosened, the talon retracting from her

flesh as the walls, the ceiling, the floor, ghosted back.

'That's her blessing,' he stammered, the spirits' howling making him stumble. 'Mortals are made that way. Time heals. Memory fades.' But not fast enough.

The nurse struck with razored nails.

The world snapped back into painful solidity as Nosplentyn sprawled on the floor, chest burning from the cut.

Her sneakers barely made a sound as she fled.

Damn it! He couldn't afford to lose her. Couldn't give the Council a reason to doubt him, to move against his family.

Nosplentyn crouched, using the pain to shore up his psychic barriers. Then he ran, following her into the 'staff only' area.

She was heading for the nearest exit. Too young or too panicked, maybe both, to simply go out a window. Falling back on human instinct and running for the stairs. Nosplentyn drew closer.

A lift door opened and an orderly appeared, pushing a trolley of linen.

The nurse dived inside the lift and Nosplentyn saw relief on her face as the doors slid shut, cutting him off. Going down. If she had the smarts, she'd stop it before ground level. Then she'd have her pick of escape routes.

Cursing, he mind-fucked the orderly, then steeled himself. This was the only way he could be certain of cutting off her escape.

He phased into the spirit world.

It was every bit as bad as he'd expected. Dark clouds of misery throbbed with bright red anguish. Scarlet bolts of agony jagged through the suffocating desolation. Spirits howled like jet engines as they flitted down midnight corridors, dodging the pale glow of plants and people projecting into the inside-out plane from the mortal side. Some still wore the shadows of their mortal faces, eyes wide with bewilderment or narrowed with anxiety. Others were little more than a screaming maw of pain and fury. They clawed at Nosplentyn's aura, confounded by his undead energy, unable to find purchase as he kept his mind resolute, his shield intact.

Nosplentyn concentrated on tracking the nurse's ghostly signature as he descended through the floors, gradually catching up. Faster! The spirits were leaching his strength. He mustn't get caught here. He couldn't let them in!

He dived through the spirit world's membrane, feeling it snap closed behind him as he re-appeared in the lift.

'How the hell did you get in here?' the nurse asked. She cowered against the wall, hands up before her. Fingernails glinted sharply.

'A gift.' He hit the emergency stop.

'Please… I could just leave town,' she pleaded.

'Too late for that. You've been noticed,' he said. 'You should've stuck to the platelets and plasma, left the living alone.'

'Processed product's not the same,' she said. 'It stills the hunger, but doesn't hold the memories, the emotions… I need those dreams! Don't you miss them?'

'Not especially.' His hardened nails sliced into his palm with the strength of his lie.

They circled in the confined space. He could smell her fear, as though the trembling lip and shaking legs weren't enough.

'I wasn't going to turn him, I swear. I know it wouldn't have cured the disease, just preserved it. Maybe made the effects even worse.'

Nosplentyn flexed his flame-scarred hand as the fingers grew into claws. He was quite aware of the limitations of the change.

'So you were just going to absorb his life force,' he said, stalking toward her. 'How kind. But what makes you think it's yours to take?'

'He would have lived on, in me,' she said, clutching her necklace.

'That's his family's job, not yours.'

'We have a gift, you and I. Why should we be the only ones who don't have to face this?' She gestured at the lift walls, but he knew what she meant.

'But we do,' Nosplentyn said. 'Everyone does. Some just sooner than others.'

He pounced, claws slashing, as she leaped to meet him…

#

Nosplentyn sat in the dented, bloody lift, numbly watching as the body burned to ash.

When he'd struck the killing blow, the rogue's life force had flashed from her body like a firework, shimmering like a miniature Milky Way with the essence of those she had devoured. She would've said 'saved', he supposed. Her spirit blasted through the poisonous cloud that was the hospital like a rocket and quickly passed from Nosplentyn's astral sight. He had no idea where it was headed. That was a mystery he would happily wait to solve. He had things to do. Overturn the Council. Reclaim his family. Find a reason to endure when so many others could not.

On his way out, he stopped at room eight in 4C. The young man still dreamed; part hoping, part dreading the arrival of his latest bone marrow biopsy. Nosplentyn touched Mr Smith's forehead and willed him past the level of dreams. He didn't need to see the test results to know the truth. But he let Mr Smith know just one thing and hoped it would lessen his grief when the results arrived. Tomorrow night, Nosplentyn would find the man's family, and when the children slept, he would anchor in their minds a single memory of their father so it would never fade. It was the only comfort he could offer; the most any mortal could hope for.

UPON THE DEAD OCEANS
Marty Young

As The USS Hodson cut through the dead ocean, I stared at the captain, stunned into silence by what he'd just told me. The words had been like an anchor to force me into the chair before him.

The weathered old man was seated at his cluttered and computer-less desk. He had stared down at the mess while speaking, almost as if the failure of which he spoke was his own doing and he couldn't bear to meet my eyes — nothing could have been further from the truth. He kept his head down now as the last echoes of his words reverberated around the small room.

Out through the tinted portholes, the ocean dipped and rose; an angry sky with swollen clouds threatening more acid rain, then deep dead waters, followed by sky again. I could feel my insides rolling with the motion, sinking with the troughs and riding the crests. The oceans were anoxic, filled with hydrogen sulphide. Even thinking about them made me feel sick.

'Jesus,' I said. It was all I had.

Captain Leahner looked up, his grey eyes rimmed with red and underlined in black. 'I used to pray to him once,' he said as he reached into a desk drawer and pulled out a bottle of dirty scotch. He unscrewed the cap and swigged from the neck, then offered it to me. 'But Jesus gave up on us a long time ago. This is the only God left that's worth praying to.'

A long time ago, too many nights now to count, scotch had

been my drink of choice. I'd had ten bottles sitting on my cabinet at home at last count; Laphroaig, Ardbeg, Penderyn, Chivas Regal, Glenfiddich — names now that meant nothing — or gave only the faintest of savoury memories.

This liquid made me cough. I wiped my lips and returned the bottle to the captain. 'New Zealand dome is at capacity so whoever goes will have to try and come back,' I said. 'You know that, right?'

'How many people were lost on your way to The Hodson?'

'Enough. Too many.'

'More than half, right?'

It was my turn to look down. I could still see their eyes as they drew and then released their last breaths, the way they just, faded, went dull, then out. The memory will never go faint though, even after all I've seen. There's no limit to the horror one can endure and recall with clarity.

'Don't carry their deaths; it'll wear you down if you do. Grind you into the dust. But get used to the feeling. You know there are no other options. That message has to get through.'

'Jesus,' I said again, looking down at my calloused hands, hands that had held so much death and now seemed destined to hold even more, because I knew he was right, damn him.

#

After the meeting, I walked back to my cabin through steel hallways, but the sounds of the ship were different, more weary, exhausted. The creaking, the groaning. The echoes. The grim looks I saw on the faces of the crew.

I fell onto my bunk. I didn't bother turning any lights on.

The Hodson was a prototype submarine-destroyer hybrid that ran on multiple power sources, capable of surface cruising as well as submerging. Its multitude of large windows had made underwater travel especially scenic before things had died. Now those windows were kept opaque so the mortuary oceans didn't crush those aboard under their oppressive weight. During surface travel, the windows were automatically turned from opaque to tint to allow a view outside while blocking the ultraviolet radiation that had killed so many, but most of us chose to keep them blackened — apart from Captain Leahner, who used the view to remind him of where we were.

I always made sure mine were blackened. I'd seen enough of that outside world.

Our survival had been sheer luck; there was no other way to describe it. When Portland Dome had gone, it had gone fast, far more quickly than any of us had believed possible. We'd thought we could patch things up enough to get us through to The Hodson's next visit, but we'd been wrong. And with no way of getting long distance messages out anymore and nowhere else to go, we had headed to the dock in the impossible hope the ship would magically be there, outside of its biannual port call.

And it had been, looking for its own miracle — but how many miracles were left in the world? Perhaps they were all extinct, too, along with hope.

The tears took me by surprise, but the pillow quickly swallowed up the sounds of my sobbing.

The wind picked up during the night and became a wild turbulent mistress to the ocean, casting its surfaces into disarray. Ghostly voices wailed about the ship, distraught at not finding a way inside to chill the blood of the men and women cowering within. Those sounds left us with visions of the dead surging alongside the vessel — God knows there was enough death to make such a ruckus.

The USS Hodson had been made to withstand much of what the seas could throw at it but it was an elderly statesman now, with arthritic limbs and cataracts in her eyes. Her joints creaked and groaned with every movement, her decks shuddered.

Sometime deep in the night, I heard the engines shut down; their hum had been a constant, a steady calming influence, a reminder of past technologies. Even under the surging ocean and wailing wind, the thrum had been there — but now that vacancy churned my stomach as much as the storm outside.

#

The next day, I met the captain at oh-eight hundred in his office as arranged. I was tired. My eyes felt gritty. The little sleep I'd managed had been filled with the tormenting dead. Faces I knew had come to glare at me through the portholes as I'd sat on my bunk, staring back.

The boat still drifted with the currents but the wild motions of last night were gone. The swell remained a good several metres so the vessel rolled from side to side, with all of its

40

aches and pains.

Captain Leahner's weathered face was set taut this morning too, and his eyes were troubled. He swayed on well-built sea legs. 'The engines failed again last night,' he said, and for the first time since I'd known him, I heard the exhaustion in his words. It was a frightening thing.

'They're still down, aren't they?'

'They've been down for the past five hours. My engineers are working on them. They're confident they can get them started again, but with the wind we had—'

'Are we lost?' I blurted, panicked by the idea of drifting endlessly in the dead oceans, being chased by howling ghosts.

'No, but we're off course. Quite some way too.' I saw his barrel chest rise as he drew in a deep breath. 'Come on, let's do what needs doing.'

'Captain—'

Leahner fixed his worn out eyes on mine. 'You choose them or I will, and then any deaths will be on you. You don't want to live with those ghosts following you, believe me.'

'But they'll never make it! We'll never make it! It's a suicide mission. It's hopeless.'

'There's always hope.'

'How can there be?'

The captain's eyes flared again. 'Because it's up to you to create it, and hold onto it, no matter what.'

I wanted to ask him how anyone could do that in a world like this, but he ushered me from his cabin out into the swaying, creaking hallway and toward the long metallic room that was the Mess. I felt as sick now as I had last night during the worst of the storm. The only hope I had was his, and I hoped it was strong enough for the both of us.

The thirty-four men and women I had spent Armageddon with were waiting for us; the captain had sent out word yesterday for them to meet us here. There were a lot of pale faces amongst that familiar rabble.

'Come close,' he called as he entered the room. My companions looked at us and in every pair of eyes I could see worry, more worry than usual. Those eyes had coloured in darkly since our trek across the mostly dead lands but there was more darkness within them now and that was some feat; I'd been certain they'd reached their limits of fear and terror a long time ago.

Some of the captain's crew had stationed themselves just within the two doorways, and even from this distance I could see the tension holding them rigid as they watched us.

'The Hodson is dying,' Captain Leahner said in his commanding voice. It was enough to still the restlessness filling the mess.

'It's falling apart and we don't have the equipment to fix it anymore. We've replaced almost every inch of this ship over the years but we've reached the end of what's possible. We've searched docks and cities, warehouses and wharfs across the world. We've done everything we could.'

There were murmurs but not much more from the ghosts of men and women before him.

'We're heading for Cape Town Dome but will first dock at New Zealand Dome so they know what's happening. We can't leave them without word. But make no mistake; this will be our last journey. Once at our final dock, everyone aboard will disembark and head for Cape Town Dome, and there we will remain, probably for ever. There will be no further connection between the three remaining domes of human civilization.'

It was obvious his words weren't new to the crew as those impressive men stood tall and proud by the doorways, but my unwilling companions were faring differently; I could see the horrified expressions spreading as the impact of what his words meant struck home.

'But how can it be failing?' Andrew Evans asked in a frightened voice. His gaunt cheeks were splotchy red; they always got that way when the man was flustered. 'It's made of titanium, isn't it?'

'There's more to the ship than just the hull. Between the water, atmosphere, and the rain, it's a surprise we've managed to keep afloat as long as we have.'

'Will we make it to Cape Town Dome if the ship's that bad?' Someone else asked — Toby McDonald, late forties, grey hair, with prominent cheek bones. He'd once been a prominent mathematician and author of five Nature papers, too — not that it mattered anymore.

'Truth is we don't know. But—'

'Then why try? Why not just dock at New Zealand Dome and stay there? You'll save a lot of death that way.'

The captain said nothing for a second, and again, I caught a glimpse of the despair within him; it was a shadow in his eye, gone before I could focus on it. It was the slow breath he drew, released before his chest could swell appreciably.

Gone in a second but the impact was much longer lasting; I

felt it swell within me, that despair, devouring the small morsel of hope he had given me back in his cabin, and leaving in its wake a bottomless dark that threatened to overwhelm me.

'If we did that,' Leahner said, 'we'd overload them, wear out their supplies and doom everyone. Do you really think we'd save any deaths that way?'

McDonald went to say something else but the captain held up his hand.

'The decision's made. But you're right; it's not going to be easy. Our magnetohydrodynamic drives are on the verge of failing for good, and when that happens, we'll be left drifting in the middle of the ocean. We'll have exhausted all available power sources by then.'

The Hodson had left port on its maiden voyage with ground-breaking and multiple energy sources, enough fuel to last decades, but the environment had changed since those days in ways no one had envisioned — and more quickly than the scientists had predicted. By rights, this damn ship should have drifted to a stop a long time ago.

'What about wind?' Toby asked.

'The weather's too unpredictable. If the mast didn't snap off through corrosion, who knows what the winds would give us. We could end up going around in circles until the bloody ship fell apart beneath us.'

The resolute old man stared around the room, meeting the looks of those before him and turning them away with his determination. There was no hint of the weight bearing down upon him anymore; whatever I'd seen was long gone. 'There's more,' he said.

I couldn't meet the stares coming from my colleagues and friends. I couldn't meet the captain's staunch look. I didn't want to be here in this room that thrummed with silent tension. Hell, I didn't want to be alive in a dead world anymore. What was the point?

'I can't afford to lose any of my crew or we won't make it anywhere, so that means it will be up to you to take the message to New Zealand Dome. You will have to make it there and back again within three days if you want to re-join us. That's the longest we can dock waiting for you.'

His words caused an uproar. Weary scientists caught in a freak of timing so long ago surged forward like an angry swell; mathematicians, geochemists and physicists, biologists and ecologists, they thundered their disapproval at the captain, who stood unmoving before them.

'It's suicide!'

'You can't expect us to do this!'

'We won't make it there and back in that time!'

'We're not soldiers; we're not trained for—'

'Enough!' Captain Leahner roared, and like that, the mess fell silent.

Right then, I wished the engines never restarted and the vessel did dissolve beneath us. I'd gladly open my mouth and drink the poisoned waters.

'Humanity is standing on the precipice and it will take the slightest of whispers to blow us over the edge. This ship is the last remaining means of transport between the domes. When it goes—'

Before he could finish what sounded like a well-used speech, one of his crew burst into the room. He was a thin wisp of a man topped with grey hair. 'Sir! Sir, you're needed on the bridge.'

The captain glared at the man but the seaman wasn't to be perturbed. 'Sir, you have to see this, it's, it's—'

I wondered if I was about to get my wish.

#

I stood next to Andrew and Toby on the port side of the enclosed deck that wrapped around the bow; this would have been a spectacular dining room in the past, offering a one-hundred and eighty degree view of the ocean. Even now we stared out at an incredible sight. The Hodson cut through waters that had an unnatural oily sheen to them, and my first thought was that the engines had finally surrendered and bled to death and I'd get my wish — but I knew that wasn't the cause.

'My God...' Andrew said next to me.

There were patches of green weed drifting alongside the vessel. Great clumps of the floating weed stretched ahead in the distance, sometimes so thick it rose up like low-lying land.

'But that's impossible,' someone said from behind me.

It was Angela Jenkins, the one-time lead biologist in the Mission to Mars project, now the failed Portland Dome. Her forehead was deeply gouged as she shook her head and stared at me. She had shaved off her grey hair long ago and kept it short. 'The scale of recovery is too fast. Impossibly fast.

You'd expect some seaweed, a few thin strands here and there maybe, but not this. It's making a complete mockery of our science.'

'Who cares about science anymore? Science didn't help when the world died, did it?' Ben Thomas, the dome's ex-head engineer, with his thick beard and worn-out eyes, he didn't even afford Angela a look; his eyes were fixed on the ever-thickening weed. 'From what I heard, extinction events like we went through should've taken thousands of years, hundreds of thousands of years. We sure as shit got that wrong, so maybe we're wrong about how quickly things recover too.'

There were murmurs of agreement from the crowd gathering along the tinted windows. Most of those standing there had long since given up their science. They drifted as aimlessly as The Hodson right now.

'Look!' Toby pointed but it wasn't necessary because the crabs were obvious, scuttling over the weed, dropping down into the waters. Their bright red and white shells were in stark contrast to the greenery of their world.

'What I'd give for fresh crab,' Andrew muttered, and his words caused a flashing cut of memory: sitting in a restaurant and being served crab curry; my wife opposite, smiling in delight at the sight of the whole crustacean sitting on a plate in a puddle of rich, spicy sauce.

But even as the memory once more seared my mind and grazed my heart, something caused the weeds to undulate; something big. The crabs froze, then darted in their curious sideways manner out of sight.

I tracked the hidden creature's progress away from us until

it sank deeper beneath the waters. Whatever it had been, it was huge. A shark? Or whale? Were there such creatures still alive in the oceans?

Or was it something new?

The Event hadn't been as terrible as the Permian extinction, but it had been bad enough. Things still lived on land and in the waters, but even over the decades since the atmosphere filled with hydrogen sulphide and the ozone layer filled with holes, those life forms had mutated into maddened blackened beasts. The oceans had remained mostly dead in that time; no plankton blooms, no sea birds flying just above the sickly waves, no fish either.

No one had seen crabs for a long time.

The murmurs filling the deck grew into excited whispering. Some of my people were crying again and their sobs were contagious. Even my throat constricted.

Was it possible? Was the world starting up again?

The weed continued to thicken until The Hodson, running on ocean currents alone, slowed to barely a crawl. The wind had died down, the swell flattening, and the floating matt of weed barely rippled. We all stood there staring at a sight none of us ever expected to see again, and the silence was complete; it was almost too much. All about us lay this mysterious weed, in places so thick it was like the banks of a massive river and we slowly navigated its course.

'I half expect to come across a derelict,' said Andrew. 'I heard the Sargasso Sea is filled with them.'

I paid him no notice; he was always going on about old books no one else was ever likely to read again.

'What's that?'

We looked around to find Jillian Armstrong, the dome's ex-medic and staunch atheist, pointing into the distance. She was skeletal these days, but then who wasn't? Food wasn't exactly abundant anymore — except for here.

I looked where she was pointing and felt my legs grow weak.

'Is that...'

The Hodson continued to drift, snagging every now and again on weed too thick to push past, its stern then swinging out and around until we were casting backwards. It was hard keeping the thing in sight, but as we drew ever closer, the trees became unmistakable.

'Trees. Living fucking trees!' Thomas cried.

He was the only one to make a sound, because the sight stole the rest of our breaths.

But the island never came any closer and we could only watch as it slipped by us on port side, swinging slowly out of sight as The Hodson navigated itself through the silent ocean of weed.

'Why aren't we stopping?' Thomas grasped me. 'We need to stop!'

I pushed him off and rushed aft in the hope of catching a final look but the view there was too restricted, and we must have passed by the thickest clumps of the weed because we didn't become snagged again. Soon, the greenery drifted into the distance, leaving us once more in dead waters.

Not long after, we heard the familiar thrum of the magnetohydrodynamic drives as they came back online. The vessel picked up speed, carrying us on toward our final destination.

#

When we made port nine days later, I was last to leave. I stood before Captain Leahner and offered the weathered old man my hand. 'Believe it or not, it was a pleasure to meet you, sir.'

I meant it. The man's courage and dedication, not to his job but to the whole of mankind, was beyond me. Whatever power source he ran on needed to be spread out amongst the debris of humanity left on this ravaged earth. Maybe then we'd truly have a chance.

'God speed, son. I hope you make it to your destination without trouble.'

'So do I.'

'We'll stretch it and give you four days, but after that, we'll have to head on. We can't afford to sit around when the vessel's falling apart around us.'

'I understand, and don't worry, we'll make it back.'

As I turned for the re-jigged gangplank, the question I'd asked myself constantly these past few weeks flared brightly in my mind again. I paused at the top, knowing I had to ask it. 'Captain, how do you do it?'

'Do what?'

'Handle living. It's kept me awake ever since you told me to choose. All I kept seeing was death for those I'd selected. How do you keep going, knowing that blood is on your hands?'

The captain didn't say anything for a long time. He looked past me, past my team organising themselves on the dock; he looked out across a desolate landscape where death ruled. His expression never changed; even behind the mask of his protective suit I could see his fierce determination.

I had the feeling that he kept a close watch on those small fractures I'd glimpsed, lest they grew too big.

'You have to hold onto hope. It's all we've got left. Hope that we're more than this, more than we've been. That our best days are yet to come. We were shown what awaits us the other day, a glimpse of what we'd lost. Now we just have to prove we're worthy of finding our way back there again.'

I looked down at the men and women waiting for me to lead them ten miles across the world toward New Zealand Dome. Ordinarily, such a distance would be an easy day's stroll, but I knew there would be losses along the way. The trailer with the oxygen tanks would take some pulling, but it was the most vital thing amongst us.

The heavy suits made them all look like astronauts, but there was no relief from gravity on this world. That was one thing that hadn't changed.

'God speed,' the captain said again. Then he turned and headed back inside his ship, back to the myriad tasks that needed doing before The Hodson would be ready to attempt its final voyage upon the dead oceans.

BEAST
Natalie Satakovski

I have heard of your paintings too, well enough; God has given you one face, and you make yourselves another.
- Hamlet

I stalk the offices like a ghost until someone needs me. When they talk to me, it's as if they're trying not to breathe. This morning at Bella Cosmetics, things are quieter than usual. I don't know, I've got a weird feeling about it.

I enter the lift with Marie whose computer I've serviced a hundred times only to be aggressively ignored on each count. She's also niece to the CEO, Louis Labelle, who hasn't approved my pay rise in eight years. I guess the genes for cruelty and beauty are inseparable. Marie's wearing that signature high ponytail of hers and I imagine myself dishevelling it. She presses the button for the seventh floor. I hit the tenth. Her basketball arse pokes out through her skirt-suit. Oh, God, I am going to die a virgin — fucking pathetic. I look up to find Marie's reflection peering from the doors, watching me.

She turns, her eyes like loaded pistols pointing at me, and moves in, so close I can smell her Dior. Suddenly she's touching me, running her fingers over the waist of my pants. But I'm an ogre, she'd never do this.

'Do you want to touch it?' she says.

I stand there, frozen. I don't understand.

Marie's petite hands tighten on my waistband, smooth fingers knuckling my gut. Then her heels click and she swings around, pushing her arse up against my crotch. My erection surges. I've seen something like this in a porno and I so badly want to find out what her cunt feels like. But there's no time. The light flashes past the 5th floor. I move to the side. Marie follows. I move back and thump into the wall, pinned by her arse.

'Stop,' I beg.

The lift chimes and the doors glide open. She sails out, flicking me one last grin. I get off the wall and feel a shift against my leg. Look down. My pants are sliding to the floor. Marie had undone them.

I cave forward in an attempt to catch my pants. Out in the open office space, people are crowding the lift. Someone gasps and female voices shrill.

Laughter.

I cower in a corner, hiding my hard-on with an arm, thumbing the 'close' button in a frenzy. The lift finally leaves.

Quarter past six. I've been waiting behind this post box for an hour and a half. I'm so high on rage my nerves are live wires. Marie will exit the building and I'll follow, wait for the chance to drag her into a dark corner, crush her skull with my bare hands.

She emerges from the revolving doors wearing a huge furry rich-bitch coat. My neck prickles. I taste hate. She stops at the curb and a cab pulls up. A guy bounces out, a real fucking prince charming, opens the door for her. Fuck. The cab cruises past and I don't try to hide. Her eyes meet mine, just for a second, before her gaze drifts away, nonchalant. The cab disappears into the traffic.

I smash the red metal with my fist.

A child's voice wafts toward me. 'Mummy, mummy, look.'

A sandy boy of about four is cowering into his mum's leg, shaking like he's just seen Sasquatch. The woman veils his face with her fingers while shooting me a concerned look.

'What's your fucking problem?' I say.

The kid screams. She picks him up and sweeps away.

#

A vertical strip of golden light. My mouth is dry and I don't know where I am. When I try to move, I realise I'm stuck, my face glued to linoleum with dried vomit. My skull splits down the middle, makes me wince. I remember. I ate a cabinet full of pharmaceuticals and I have to laugh inside because I'm still alive. Antihistamines could have prevented the vomit reaction, but I was so desperate I didn't bother to go out for some. Rookie mistake.

There's no way I can report what happened in the lift. The last time I tried to approach authority was in high school. The beautiful kids used chewing gum to stick thumb tacks onto my seat. Though I ended up developing an infection and bleeding through my pants for a week after, the principal laughed and told me it was all in good fun.

I'm not going to work tomorrow. I'm not going back to

Bella Cosmetics, or anywhere, ever again.

A knock at my door.

Fuck it. I won't answer.

'Damien?'

It's a woman's voice muffled through the wood. The shadow of her head bobs through the opaque glass.

'Damien. Are you home?'

Rocket. She must have noticed my car in the drive and wondered why I wasn't at work. Probably come over to check on me. She knocks again and her dark caramel voice calls my name once more. It shatters me, my face starts steaming with tears.

If I open the door, I'll have to explain myself. If I don't, maybe I can try this again and do it properly.

Please go away, Rocket. This is none of your business.

The shadows of her feet shift beneath the door. They grow into the shape of her thigh and she's kneeling down, lowering her head to peer inside.

#

Rocket emerges from the kitchen with a tea pot while I wallow on the couch, wrapped in a towel.

I call her Rocket because of a game we used to play as kids. Although we were the same age, I was much bigger than her. I'd lie on my back and use my feet as a seat for her. I'd push my legs up, propelling her out onto a sea of cushions. I was the launcher, she was the rocket. My first cousin — and the only person who's ever been nice to me — now lives in the same

55

apartment block.

'Do you need me to drive you to the doctor's?' she asks.

I tell her I'm fine.

Rocket wipes sticky hair from my forehead. It tingles and I freeze up because so few people have touched me and because I repulse myself. Her kindness is humiliating.

'I can stay if you need me,' she says.

I tell her I'll be fine.

#

I'm sitting in front of my PlayStation when there's a knock at my door. That's funny, I haven't ordered pizza today. And the only time I hear that sound is if Rocket comes to visit — the only person I've seen in two weeks. I peek past the curtains but it isn't her. It's a girl of about sixteen. She's one of those Disney princesses: skirt so short it's enticing but not enough to be slutty; golden locks untainted by chemical hair dye. She's a natural beauty. She doesn't need to hide behind mascara or foundation; just a bit of day cream from the Bella Naturals line and some cherry lip gloss to set off her eyes. She's even got that high pony tail. No way am I going to open for that bitch.

The girl rings a second time. Maybe she's a little older, twenty even. What's she got? The box must contain chocolates for a fundraiser. Doesn't make her a good person, but perhaps she's more humane than the rest. I could open up and get a better look at her. And I'm really craving sugar. Worst case scenario, I get new files for the wank bank.

I unlock the deadbolt and open the door to look at her

through the mesh of the screen. She can't see me clearly, smiling vaguely in the direction she thinks my head might be. I push the screen door open.

As she steps back, my consciousness pivots from my body to hers, and I see myself as she must see me. Towering two heads above her, ghoulish features glow from the dimmed interior of the hall, brow so low over beady eyes I look permanently enraged. No wonder people hate me; people hate what they fear.

The girl glances at the box she's holding and then back at me.

'Yes?' I say.

'I think,' she says at last, 'I've got the wrong house.'

'Aren't you just selling chocolate?' I keep my eyes dead on hers.

She clutches the box to her chest. 'No, I'm not. Sorry to bother you.'

She turns. That little fucking over-sized girl scout is about to walk away. Because I'm too ugly to be sold chocolates. Too ugly to be treated like a fucking human being going about their life in the most unobtrusive way, holed up in this fucking shoebox so as not to cause a nuisance to the world with my hatefulness. No human contact for thirteen fucking days and now this. I get a flashback to Marie's grin, the lift. My blood percolates and rage takes over.

I grab Girl Scout by the arm. She screams.

I yank her toward me. She trips, slamming her head on the door frame. For a second, she staggers, keeling over at a right angle. I grab her head and smash it into the brick wall. She crumples to the floor.

The car park is empty. I drag her and the box inside. Shut the door.

Blood beats in my throat and roars in my ears. I'm so angry I can't even think. I only want to destroy her, recompense for everyone who's laughed at me. I kick her. She moans and my cock throbs. I stand there for a moment wondering if I want to kill her or fuck her. I decide that first I'm gonna eat some goddamn chocolate. I pick up the box and get a surprise. Instead of bars of Cadbury Dairy Milk and stupid cancer pins: jars. I take one out. 'Natural moisturiser'. Shit, she was right. The little twat was telling the truth after all.

I panic.

She's limp on the carpet, face veiled by loosened hair. I'm in deep shit for this. No matter what I do, I'll get jail time for assault. Maybe I can get rid of her, get away with it. I'll chop her up and put her into the garbage disposal piece by piece before the cops show up to question me. My life's turned to rot regardless, so what have I got to lose?

I drag the cunt into the bathroom and lug her into the tub. Her head falls back, eyes rolling around like marbles. I rush blindly to the kitchen for a knife. This is it. I have to act now before she comes to. I press the blade to her throat and look away. Blood sprays out like water from a partially clogged faucet. She spasms in the tub, back and limbs drumming against the enamel.

What have I done? My hands are brown with blood. I turn the tap on to scrub them clean and realise that I've left the plug in the basin. Red water rises around her thighs. It stinks like wet coins, so strong I can taste it. Can't get the blood off my hands. It's everywhere. I turn the tap off. My vision blurs, but when I try to wipe the tears away, I get blood in my eyes. Shit. I've finally fucked up, really fucked up. I'm never going to get away with this. *Beast Slays Beauty in Suburban Horror.* I'm going to spend the rest of my life in jail.

How did I end up here? Why couldn't I have been born normal like everyone else? I'd give anything to look like them. Like the kiddies who'd had the luxury of ostracising me as a child, and the perfect couples on trains who gawk at me and whisper and giggle. Like the people at Bella Cosmetics, and that King-dick Louis Labelle, CEO and managing director, that arrogant prick who built his fortune on ideals of beauty that I can never live up to. It's those ideals that cause others to hate me and laugh at me and treat me like shit. What would the world be like without people like him? There would be no beauty, and there would be no misery for me.

I can either sit around with the dead girl, watching maggots eat her out while I wait for the cops to bust me. Or I can spend my last few hours of freedom on reprisal. I may as well go out with a bang.

I take a shower and put on my best suit. I empty the jars of moisturiser over Sleeping Beauty's face and then dunk each one into the pool of blood, watching them fill with a gulp.

As I lock the front door, I realise it probably isn't necessary — they're going to catch me by the time this is through. I'm struggling to pull this dodgy key out when Rocket's car pulls up in the driveway. Shit. She's going to ask me where I'm going. Why is she always sticking her face into my business?

Oh, Rocket. I know you're not like the rest of them, but I hate everyone and I'm going to do this.

Pretending like I haven't seen her, I walk toward my car.

'Damien,' she calls out. I don't know if I can make it to my car before she intercepts. Keep my head down.

'Hey, where are you going?'

A few more paces and I'll be there.

'Damien, stop.' Her voice changes from that smooth husk into a whining plea. 'Why are you ignoring me?'

Her hand reaches out. I snatch it and throw it back at her, sending her body shuddering away. The frailty of her movement reminds me of the dead girl. Guilt pierces my chest.

I get into my car.

Rocket's gawking where I left her. 'Fuck you then!'

In my rear view mirror, her face is contorted with tears, partly masked by one hand, the other cradled around her chest.

#

These offices are so stylish it makes me sick. The fleur-de-lis carpet and purple walls radiate hostility. I never belonged here. I treat the people like video game obstacles, and imagine myself in a first-person shooter, knocking them off as I make my way though. Maybe I'll try that on my way out, after killing the prize target.

I haven't been here for two weeks and everyone's staring at me. Someone laughs and says, 'Come to beg for your job back, ey?'

I raise my head and see a man about a foot shorter than me.

His eyes widen and lips seal up when he sees my face. I continue through.

Labelle's office is empty. Once inside, I pull the blinds closed and wait at his desk, propping my briefcase on the polished wood. I rub nervous track marks into the rug.

The door clicks and Labelle strides in. I feel a gust of air as he zips past me.

'Yes?' he says. 'Who are you and what do you want?'

He knows me. I see the recognition in his face. He just never cared to learn my name.

I stand up, wanting to seem confident, important. He looks up at me without craning his neck, defiant. I mutter an introduction, shaking so badly I'm afraid to hold my hand out.

'I've got a new product that may interest you,' I say. 'I've come to discuss business prospects.'

Labelle skims my suit and says, 'Look, I'm really sorry but we can't think about new products right now. We're busy trying to launch the new range we've spent the past two years developing. I appreciate your time but maybe you can get in touch with another company to manufacture your... *product* for you.'

My knife is in my briefcase. If I can just get him to sit down and look at the jars, then I can pull it out and slash his throat.

'But you don't understand,' I say.

He squints, tacking me to the wall.

'My product is special,' I say. 'Mr Labelle, you're the CEO of this prestigious company and a true connoisseur of cosmetics. Why not take a seat and have a look for yourself? If after seeing my product you're still not interested, I'll trust your judgment. But please, don't say no before you try it.'

He can see me trembling. He's going to throw me out.

He exhales and sits down. 'Okay.'

I sit opposite and open the briefcase. Slowly, I retrieve one of the blood jars, and pass it to him with two hands. He takes the brown-red jar, twisting it around to read the label. The label's stained and peeling but still reads *Natural Moisturiser*.

He looks at me as if to ask, *What the hell is this?*

'Please.' I gesture for him to go ahead.

His fingers tighten around the lid and it pops open. That tinny smell envelops us. Nose twitching, he brings it in for closer scrutiny and sniffs.

I lift the knife with two fingers and ease it into my grip.

Labelle looks at me again — surely he must recognise that it's full of blood. But instead of looking horrified, he seems puzzled.

I'm trembling so bad that the knife rattles against the briefcase.

'What is it?' he asks.

I'm delirious with nerves. I suddenly have the urge to tell him. I want to see his reaction.

'Virgin's blood,' I say. Screaming inside, *Now! Do it now!* but I'm paralysed.

His eyebrows crease. Labelle leans forward. I think he's going to puke. He whispers, 'Is it pure?'

I drop the knife, making a tiny thud.

I croak. He stares.

I say the first thing that comes to mind. 'It's mixed with water.' He's still staring, so I quickly add, 'A precise ratio of about one part blood to four parts distilled water — the recommended ratio for a truly lavish and nourishing virgin blood bath.'

He nods and taps the desk with a pen. 'I'm certainly interested in this exquisite moisturiser. Here I was thinking 'bloody Bathory' products were a myth. Listen, we are not secure discussing business here.'

He presses a button on his phone and speaks into the receiver. 'Jenny. Cancel my three-thirty and make sure I have no interruptions. I'm in a very important meeting.'

The world's swirling all around me yet I'm completely still inside. I don't know if my heart's stopped working or if I've finally reached nirvana.

Labelle says, 'Please, sir. Come this way.'

I creak out of the seat, knees untrustworthy. He leads me to another room, which I'm guessing none but the highest company management know about. In the middle, two velvet armchairs bookend a marble coffee table, behind them a mantelpiece runs along the wall space. Labelle offers me a seat while he stands by the mantel.

'At Bella,' he says, 'we supply first class cosmetics to boutiques and high-end department stores worldwide. We provide makeup for films and fashion shows, and we have the most glamorous supermodels associated with our brand. But we also have a line of products far removed from the public eye. Handcrafted, secret innovations that have unparalleled powers to beautify, polish and preserve. We eschew the ethical and legal confines that hinder innovation. We employ uninhibited scientists and give them the resources to test, torture and invent, to channel the real powers behind effective cosmetic treatment. Here, just behind these walls, is a lab where genius is limitless.'

He turns to the shelf and takes a parcel wrapped in brown paper.

'These soaps have been made from the finest tallow. Can you guess which animal it comes from? For a long time, we believed seal cubs had the most luxurious fatty tissue. That was until a Peruvian entrepreneur slaughtered a mass of choice native girls to produce this. We've gone into business with him to expand this line to include shaving foam and body gel.'

He holds the package out to me but I can't take it. I have to use all my willpower not to scream. Labelle, still holding the product out to me, hesitates, then places it on the table.

He returns to the shelf and takes a porcelain cylinder.

'Please, try some of this anti-aging serum. You'll find it is rapidly absorbed into the skin, leaving a light and wonderful fragrance. It was formulated with the most potent elastins known to modern science — from infant foreskins.'

I'm thinking, *You are a monster. You are Hell on Earth.*

He puts the foreskin oil next to the package. 'Please accept these as gifts.' All of a sudden staring at me, piercing me. Why's he looking at me like that?

'I think you'll find, sir,' he continues, 'that these products are much more than just skincare.'

Labelle's thick hand pats my back. I try not to let my shoulders tense but they're crawling with insects.

'Let me fix us a drink,' he says. 'Do you appreciate good bourbon?'

While he's gone, I browse the items on the mantel. I pick up a canister styled as a Japanese temple. Does this crap actually work? I feel weak. I've lost my energy to kill Labelle though I despise him more than ever. What if I make a deal with Bella and get some money? I could spend it on a hooker and mounds of cocaine then blow my brains out and die with my balls empty. Or I could flee the country. Apologise to Rocket, ask her to come with me.

Labelle returns holding a pair of crystal glasses. I agree to provide Bella with virgin's blood at a price of $3999.99 per litre, which they will package and distribute to an underground market of trusted clientele. Labelle sets me up at a luxury villa at the Casino, covering all my expenses. I've never been treated like this. It makes me ashamed, guilty that I enjoy it.

He holds out his hand for me to shake. And for the first time in my life, I don't feel like a hideous freak.

#

This fluffy queen-sized bed is so clean and crisp it reminds me of Rocket's underwear fresh off the clothes line. Last night, I drank a bottle of room-service cognac and lathered myself in every complimentary product given to me by Labelle. Expensive wrapping paper and potion-like bottles make a trail from bed to bathroom. Someone is banging on the door and I realise what has woken me.

'Damien Elgar? Open up. Police.'

I rise like a corpse from a coffin. Directly ahead of me, I catch my reflection in the bathroom mirror. My eyes don't seem to be working. I wonder what else I consumed other than alcohol. The fist hammers at the door again, but I ignore it.

Feet on cold tiles, I look at myself up close. Everything's changed. My once protruding forehead seems to have receded to a gentle brow. I grope my face and find that my skin, which has always been thick and porous, is now supple and smooth. And I don't even remember what my lips looked like before, because now they're smiling at me, handsome.

The cops are banging on the door. But I don't care. Whoever they are after, it is no longer me.

THE GRINNING TIDE
Stuart Olver

The land shuddered, floundered in its shallow grave between ancient granite ridges, its barrel-chested hills choking on white crystalline dust. Like a corpse, not knowing its own death, trying to rise while the gravedigger sprinkles salt and pounds with his spade. The mallees, brown and hunched, overtaken by the creeping white tide, and the ghosts of fluted gums raising stripped branches from the brine-scarred earth, like furious fingers clawing at the salt-scoured sky. And Gary's lone, red Camry on the highway, lost in the vastness of the landscape, little more than a drop of blood oozing slowly along a dead, black vein.

The arrow-straight stretch of road would probably have claimed Gary's life that day if the girl hadn't made a run at him. Some beers at lunch (he couldn't remember if he'd stopped at two, as he'd promised himself he would) and a warm and stuffy car had conspired to bring him to the brink of unconsciousness. So too, the unremarkable plains of the wheatbelt unfolding flat as a map twenty kilometres out from Kellerberrin. The girl was a sudden flash of white, agitating the edges of his vision, causing him to step on the brake too hard.

The car shimmied to a stop in the gravel. Gary glanced back, not at all convinced he hadn't clipped the slim figure. But there she was, a few metres back, hurrying toward the passenger door. Gary lowered the electric window as her face, pink-cheeked and grime-smudged, drew level with it.

'You gotta help me, mister. My pop… he's very sick.'

Gary stared at the girl. She was about eleven or twelve; her white dress, though clean, bore the frayed marks of continual use.

'Your grandfather?'

'Yeah. He's gonna die for sure. Please come.'

'Where is he?'

'At the house. Down the road.'

She pointed backwards to a narrow bitumen track, lined with rickety fence posts and slack lengths of wire that led off to the left from the main road. Gary was briefly surprised he had not noticed it before, but then again, he'd barely been aware of the road he was travelling on until a few seconds ago.

'At a farmhouse?'

'Yeah, mister. Hurry!'

Gary frowned and leaned over to open the passenger door for the girl.

Lucy would have been about the same age…

'Get in. I'll drive us down.'

The girl shuffled into the seat, and Gary did a U-turn and steered the car down the secondary road.

'Where are your parents?' he asked.

'They went away.'

'What do you mean 'they went away'?'

'That's it. They went down the fields, and they didn't come back yet.'

'Who's looking after you?'

'My pop, of course. Jeez, you ask a lot of questions, mister.'

The car rumbled along the road, and the twisting wire and rotting fence posts framed vast salt pans in the dying wheat stubble, like spreading white mould sneezed onto a thousand-acre Petri dish. The sun threw its rays, hot and thick, through the left side windows, though Gary noticed a line of cumulus clouds forming up on the horizon ahead, merging like a creamy breaking wave getting ready to rush forward onto the sand.

'Looks like we could get a storm,' he said, because the silence made him anxious. He nervously rubbed the ring finger on his left hand, a habit he still could not break after all this time.

'Won't be nothing but lightning,' said the girl, 'lightning and a whole lot of clouds crashing about, and maybe they'll throw down some ice, but what's the good of that? 'Cos you can't stand out in the hail and catch it on your tongue, can you?'

Gary glanced quickly at the girl. She had a petulant look on her face, but it only made her seem younger and more vulnerable. He thought back to the pub where he'd stopped for lunch. The men huddled over their beers, and the way the beer tap sputtered, and the cloudy lager it produced.

'You guys must be really struggling out here,' he said. The girl merely looked away out the window.

Some ten minutes passed before the girl called suddenly, 'Left here.' There was a fork in the road, and Gary branched left and they immediately ran off the bitumen. The dirt track carried them toward a small rise, and bare granite scalloped away on either side until they stuttered over a cattle grid, the last of the trees fell away, the ridge was crested, and the unclothed land spread out before them. Yellow grass tufted the brown soil all the way to the single wooden farmhouse, then disappeared beyond it, replaced by hundreds of termite mounds. They glittered as if constructed of equal parts salt and mud, and pierced the cracked bare earth in all directions.

Gary eased the car down the steep last few metres of the track. The tyres gripped the dirt hard, as if clawing the ground in an effort to retreat, and the engine surged, its whine like that of a dog being dragged on a leash. Finally, Gary brought the Camry to a stop outside the house, and cut the ignition. The sudden silence was like a stifled scream. No bird calls greeted him as he opened his door, no breeze hummed against the drooping gutters of the house, no trees crackled in the afternoon heat haze. Gary pointed at the rundown farmhouse and the termite mounds.

'What happened here?' he said. 'Don't you have any irrigation?'

The girl startled Gary by grabbing his hand and pulling him along. 'Hurry! Pop's over here.'

She led him onto a creaking stoop, then through an open doorway into a corridor that ran the length of the house, which was only a few metres. Then they were out into the sunshine at the back and Gary's eyes struggled to adjust to the harsh whiteness of the light, which saturated the scene as if he was looking at a washed out photograph: a verandah shaded by a trellis of tattered passionfruit vine, a few lumpy couches piled high with clothes, a warped coffee table with a broken ashtray, several buckets, a pickaxe, a hacksaw, piles of old books, brown and brittle plants in pots, a box of broken toys. In one corner hung a large wooden box, two of its opposing sides open to the air but covered by fine plastic mesh. Inside the box were hung strips of something dark and leathery. Gary had to stare at them for several seconds before he realised they were strips of drying jerky.

'Over here, mister.'

The girl again took his hand, and led him toward the couch on the left. At first, he could not distinguish anything apart from a jumble of clothes and a discarded mop head, but then the items shifted, seemingly by themselves, and Gary noticed something thin, wrinkled and brown lying half hidden under a shirt. In fact, it had its origin inside the shirt, and emerged through a sleeve. The mop head lifted, revealing an ancient wrinkled face, and Gary realised he'd found the girl's grandfather.

'Pop... Pop...' said the girl as she gave the old man's shoulder a good shake, 'Get up!'

The man simply stared up at her, his eyes blinking, once, twice. The girl leaned over him, tucked her arms under his armpits, and pulled him upright. He came up easily, as if he weighed almost nothing. His shirt hung loosely, the neck open almost to his navel, exposing leathery skin stretched over ribcage.

'I'll bring you drink, pop,' said the girl, speaking slowly and miming the action of raising a glass to her lips, as though speaking to a child. She dashed inside, leaving Gary to stare at the old man, who gazed wide-eyed back at him, his lips quivering and his fingers trembling. Gary heard a *phut phut* sound from inside the house, and a harsh juddering of pipes. The girl emerged, carrying a glass filled with grey liquid. Sediment had already begun to collect at the bottom.

'You can't give him that,' said Gary, sure that he could actually see little wriggling things in the liquid.

'This is all that comes out the taps,' said the girl defensively. 'Why don't you try if you think you can do better?'

'Actually, I can do better,' said Gary. 'I've got an almost full water container in the back of the car. I'll go get it.'

He left the girl standing there and fetched the water. As he stumbled back out on to the back porch, hugging the heavy container to his chest, he was startled to see the girl tilting her grandfather's head back and attempting to force liquid from the glass down his throat.

'Hey, don't do that!' he shouted, and he dropped the water container onto the coffee table and moved to grab the glass from the girl's hand. She shrank back, her teeth bared like a cornered beast.

'You'll make him sick,' said Gary. 'Look, I've got clean water now.' He held out his hand, and the girl reluctantly handed the glass to him.

'Have you got some dishwashing liquid?' The girl shook her head. 'Some soap?' The girl shrugged.

Gary grunted impatiently, and unscrewed the cap of the plastic container. He tipped water into the glass, swirled it around, and emptied it onto the dusty concrete, before repeating the whole process. Finally, he filled the glass almost to the brim, crouched down next to the girl's grandfather, and raised the glass gently to his salt-rimmed lips. The man slurped hesitantly, then with increasing vigour, so that the water ran down over his chin and spattered on the clothes covering his lap. He looked at Gary, his eyes springing wide open, and suddenly his two scrawny arms shot up and grabbed Gary firmly around the waist. The glass slipped to the ground and shattered. Gary tried to prise the old man's arms loose, but they seemed to have spasmed tight around him. The man brought his face up to within centimetres of Gary's. His mouth opened wide to reveal rotting teeth and a stench like sour milk lay hot and heavy on his breath.

'Wah... waaahh...' He appeared to be trying to talk, but Gary could not make out a single word. He gripped the old man's shoulders and used all his strength to shove him away; the man's eyes grew wide with fear, and a high-pitched babble tumbled from his lips as he suddenly toppled back violently, clothes slipping from his lap. Gary stared in horror as two raw stumps appeared where the man's legs should have been; something hit the side of his left knee, eliciting an immediate spike of pain, and a sound like a branch snapping.

Screaming in agony, Gary fell back in time to see the girl wrestle the point of the pickaxe from his shattered knee. Red-cheeked and grunting, she strained to raise the tool again, before swinging it clumsily and ineffectually at Gary's head. The head of the pickaxe hit the ground, and the girl leaned on the handle, breathing heavily. When she lifted her face, Gary saw that she had begun to cry.

'I'm sorry, mister… I'm sorry…'

'My knee's broken!' gasped Gary. 'I have to get to a hospital.' He gripped his leg as it began to throb and clamped a hand against the blood trickling from the wound, ratcheting the pain in his knee so high that he almost passed out. He steadied his head with sticky hands and then used his right to fish around in his shorts pocket for his mobile. As he pulled it out, the girl took a step toward him and raised the pickaxe again.

'Give it to me!' she said, her face twisting with sudden anger. 'Give it to me or I'll bash your brains in!'

Gary threw the phone at her. She snapped her head back, but it hit her anyway, on the left cheekbone. She lost her grip on the pickaxe and it clattered to the ground. Gary tried to propel himself forward, but a jagged edge of pain along his left leg left him gasping and floundering in a heap on the floor some three feet from her. She recovered quickly, hoisting the pickaxe again, and bringing it down on Gary's phone, which shattered immediately. Gary levered himself up with his arms, but this time the girl closed in quickly, with two hands firmly clamped on the handle of the pickaxe. She pounded its head into his chin.

The world inverted; the trellis trailing its dead vines wavered hazy and indistinct, in a sky that seemed to be darkening like coffee grounds swirling through scalding water. He felt only a heaviness that pain could not penetrate, and the girl's hands under his shoulders, dragging him, stopping, dragging him again…

Then, for a while, nothing mattered, though he saw shapes

flit like shadows across his vision, with a sound in his ears like sand scuffing grass on windblown dunes. His lips tasted wetness, and he struggled to swallow, dimly aware that someone was tipping water down his throat. He couldn't breathe, briny water flooding his lungs, vomiting back up again, streaming from his mouth, and his wife was there, her face streaming, sobbing, choking with rage.

You were supposed to be watching her!

And he was helpless; what useless words…

But this is normally such a calm beach.

He tried to move his arms, but they were shackled somehow behind his back. And as the memory of where he was returned, so did awareness of the throbbing pain in his left knee.

He was seated on an old armchair a few metres from the couch on which the girl's grandfather sat upright once more. The girl leaned over Gary, bringing a glass full of dirty water toward his mouth, and he knew that the water was sickening him. For though the sun still sent the full force of its rays against his skin, its face was black, and the sky surrounding it glowed silver. Thunderheads menaced the horizon, piling up, churning closer, snagging out lightning like flicking snakes' tongues. Rain squalled a section of the barren termite-scape in the middle distance, shrouding it with grey mist.

The girl squealed in delight.

'You brought the water!' she said, forcing his mouth open with a violent shove of the glass against his lips. Gary choked and spat, looked at the approaching rain, and realised the girl was not talking about the water he'd fetched from the car. She turned and faced the edge of the verandah, her face glowing and ravenous, as the storm closed in with frightening ferocity, finally quenching the dead sun, and with its arsenal of fat rain drops began to tear apart the plain of termite mounds. The clay cratered and crumbled as the water gouged out little plumes of dust, and the soil coalesced, slid in little rivulets like creeping amoebas. The bones, the hidden bones, showing through the claggy mess, emerging white and gleaming like fossils in the sluice; the rattling bones, skulls and shoulder blades and ribs and pelvis, snapping together like some child's construction kit; the legs, freed and moving, stepping forward, dragging each skeleton with mud hanging off like bits of flesh.

Skeletons of kangaroos and wallabies with elongated tibias and drawn-out tails, dingoes with broad, flat skulls and mighty teeth, lumbering cattle and sheep with large, curved mandibles, rodents and lizards and snakes, and scattered in amongst them all, the erect bones of humans.

The rain washed away the termite mounds, one by one, and one by one, the fleshless corpses staggered toward the verandah.

The girl's grandfather began to shake, nameless words tumbling from his lips like some frenzied preacher. The girl stood on the edge of the verandah, arms spread to the rain, her tongue darting out to spoon up the droplets that spattered her face. She lifted her head, exultant at each lightning strike. The disinterred bones passed by her, ignored her; clattering and skittering they rushed in like the tide toward the old man. They churned against him, skeleton upon skeleton, bone piled high upon bone until he was covered, and consumed, and his whimpering ceased. Then the great cresting wave broke, and the bones surged back off the concrete and onto the sodden plain, gradually disentangling to form up again as distinct skeletons, which moved apart to take up positions at irregular intervals in the mud. Then, as one, they turned so that their grinning skulls looked directly at Gary.

Of the old man, there was not a trace.

The girl scampered around in the rain, placing buckets to catch the water, which she then tipped into an old cement washtub. She finally turned back onto the verandah, her face shiny and her dress sodden. She walked up to Gary and gazed down at him.

'I would have been next, you see,' she said.

The rain continued all that night, and Gary dozed fitfully in his semi-seated position. The lightning jagged him awake often, imprinting the image of hundreds of staring eye sockets on his mind. He became convinced the skeletons were edging closer to him as the night wore on. And as the eastern horizon merged black upon grey about an hour before dawn, he was sure he could see Lucy walking whole amongst the bones. But when she came closer, he could see her face was half ruined, and she called out to him in a voice that rattled and frothed.

Why did you bring the water, daddy?

Gary fell into a deep faint, and when he awoke, the orange sun was sculpturing shadows from the termite mounds, dry and whole once again. He wavered on the edge of consciousness as the sun carried the day to its apex. The barren plain with its clay sentinels baked and shimmered, and the sky was such a brittle blue that it seemed it might shatter at any instant. A terrible hunger and thirst grew in him, but all the girl brought him was brackish water and salty jerky. Even these he began to crave before long, convinced that the poisoned waters of the aquifer that the deluge had brought to the surface were flowing into his body, and crystallizing in his cells.

And all the while, the ravenous, dying land gazed upon him, licking its lips, waiting for a storm to sharpen its teeth.

And for the bones to surge forward once more.

OUR LAST MEAL
J. Ashley Smith

It used to be our favourite lookout. Our hangover lookout, Sallie had called it.

We always got trashed the night we arrived, and the next day, would roll out of the cabin before dawn, woken by the kookas outside the bedroom and the painful clarity crystallising behind our eyes. We'd slog our way through the rainforest, sweating poison, Sallie forever in the lead, boasting how she'd walked this track since she was a toddler and couldn't I keep up. At the top, we'd stretch out on the coarse rock and share the same, unchanging picnic: crackers, cheese, and cucumber sliced with a knock-off Swiss Army penknife, all rinsed back with the warm dregs of last night's bottle of white. And there we would lose ourselves, gazing out across the canopy below and the hazy blue exhalations that rose above it, into the deeper blue of the sky.

It could never be the same without her; I knew that. But something had drawn me back here to spread out that same simple lunch and stare blankly at those same treetops. I'd invested in a bona fide Swiss Army knife since then, and was washing down the food with water instead of wine — I had only ever got drunk because Sallie had. But whatever it was I had hoped to recapture remained hidden, or had never been there to begin with.

There had been a storm in the night and the rainforest that

morning steamed, lush with the smells of life giving birth to itself without cease. The foliage all about me resonated with the calls of whip birds and whistlers, the rustlings of scrub turkeys, and of other creatures too innumerable to distinguish or identify; and of creatures too small or silent to acknowledge.

My feet were swollen from the walk, and aching. Trickling streams of ants converged on the crumbs of crackers and the flakes of cheese. I unlaced my boots and tugged them off, surprised to find my left sock was dark and soaking. As I peeled it off, my hand came away smeared with a watery redness. I rolled up my trouser cuff to uncover the wound and found instead a leech, bloated and quivering.

It was as round as my thumb and twice as long, shiny black with streaks of orange. Even as I watched, it seemed, with each of its hideous pulsations, to be getting larger.

I'm ashamed to admit it now, but I was so overcome with revulsion that I panicked. In an instant, I was on my feet, kicking at the air. I wanted it off me, but I couldn't bring myself to touch it. I flicked at it spastically, trying to brush it away, but the leech held on, its engorged body flapping against my calf like a bloody balloon.

It would have drawn some odd looks, had there been anyone around to see it: a bearded young man hopping barefoot on the rocks, arms flailing against an outstretched leg, while his twisted mouth strangled noises of disgust. I can laugh about it now, but at the time I had no sense of how daft I must have looked. Only the hysterical thought voicing itself over and over: It is drinking me!

In the end, the leech just let go. Engorged and rippling, it writhed among the remains of my ritual lunch.

Something welled up in me then, something I could not contain. I picked up my boot by the toe and slammed the heel down on the leech.

That first blow had no effect, so I struck again. And again, and again, and again. I felt the reverberation in my arm each time the sole struck rock. I was grunting. Jaw clenched. Teeth grinding.

When I finally stopped, I was panting, almost in tears. There was nothing left of the leech but a twist of black, like a burnt elastic band, and a burst of red the size of my palm, pooling in the striations of the rock.

My blood.

#

All the way back to the cabin, I was consumed with disgust.

The walk seemed longer than usual, and more perilous. I recoiled from every frond that brushed my calves, jumped at each drop of water that fell from the canopy above. The rainforest teemed with life-forms of every sort, both real and imagined. Every path was criss-crossed with the giant webs of orb spiders. Every leaf was crawling with the black bodies of sucking, biting parasites. I swept and lashed at every sensation — on my arms, my neck, my shins. Every exposed patch of skin seemed to be alive with creeping crawling things.

Before I finally passed through the gates of the national park, I had removed three more leeches from my boots. It was an enormous relief to feel the concrete beneath me again: man-made, impervious, reassuringly lifeless.

But the disgust stayed with me.

It was a feeling I knew well, however indirectly. In the months before she left, I had seen it creep across Sallie's face like a shadow, seen it pull down the edges of her mouth, seen it in the way she turned from me, as though unable to bear the sight of me any longer.

'It's like living with a black hole,' she had said.

And then: 'I hate who I am with you.'

And then: 'You're draining the life from me.'

It made no sense to me. I heard the words, but it seemed she was talking about some other person — someone I did not recognise and could not identify with.

In the time we'd been together, I'd done all I could to become the perfect partner. I was dedicated to her constant happiness, moulding myself precisely to each contour of her personality. Every quality she disliked in a man — vanity, aggression, jealousy, protectiveness — I erased from myself as though they had never been. Her likes became mine. Her interests and opinions too. I cooked her favourite foods, met up with her friends in her favourite bars, massaged her feet to her favourite movies. I wanted everything to be perfect for her, for every one of our moments together to be a festival of worship, a religious devotion with her the central deity.

But as I came close to that idea of perfection on which I'd staked everything, Sallie began to change. That shadow fell across her eyes. That twist appeared at the corner of her mouth. Finally, there came the looks of unmistakable contempt.

'But I love you,' I had said.

'You love something,' she said. 'But it isn't me.'

'And you? Do you…?' I couldn't bring myself to say it.

'Do I love you?' she said, and looked at me as though at a complete stranger. 'What's there to love?'

Sallie and I continued to live together for some weeks after that, but we were just bodies drifting through a vacuum: all coldness and silence and the mounting fear of suffocation. I went through the motions, carrying on as though nothing had changed, perhaps believing that those words could be undone or overpowered by the simple repetition of established habits. But the change was written on her face. The twist grew into a sneer and, soon enough, I had to accept that it was over.

Within days of moving out, Sallie started seeing her ex, the one that I had worked so hard to be nothing like. Shortly after, she set off for Europe on some pseudo-existential jaunt; to 'find herself', perhaps, or to put as much distance as she could between her and me.

I thought I had made myself exactly what she needed me to be. But in the end, it just wasn't enough. Or wasn't what she had wanted in the first place.

#

The cabin was a basic affair, characterised by its size and lack of amenity; two small bedrooms, a smaller bathroom, and combined kitchen-living room, were compressed together beneath an old tin roof. It stood empty most of the year, so had become a home to every imaginable sort of vermin. I was kept awake each night by the rattle of possums across the roof and the skittering of rats in the walls, then deprived of sleep past dawn by the scratch of claws on tin and the cacophony of shrieks as cockatoos drove smaller parrots from the feeder. The back deck looked out upon the garden: a wild tangle of rainforest from which, at night, the faraway lights of the Gold Coast could be seen, shimmering through giant fronds of cycads and bursts of frangipani like a hallucination.

The cabin and surrounding block had been in Sallie's family for years. Her parents had bought it before she was born, in the carefree early days of their marriage. It was unique on this road of stately Queenslanders, of expansive and manicured gardens; a little island of wilderness that her parents swore always to keep intact, never to develop. It had been their family retreat throughout Sallie's childhood, and later, when she and her brother were at uni, it had been their escape, a free space for their group's riotous weekends or an intimate one for their lovers. Her brother married and moved to Perth and her parents had followed to be closer to their grandchildren. For some time, Sallie and I had been the cabin's only visitors.

In the first flush of our romance, we had come often, whiling away the days in blissful aimlessness. We would walk the local bush trails, loving the exhaustion and the closeness that came with it. Long, impassioned siestas in the heaviness of afternoon would drift into boozy dinners on the verandah, watching the night descend into the spatter of lights that marked the coastline. In those happier times, the cabin was our haven, a cocoon in which the best parts of ourselves felt safe to emerge, and love, with all its possibilities, could grow without restraint.

In the cold last days, however, the only retreats we made were into our own private worlds, and the cabin remained empty. We still walked, but only to work, and separately, immersed in the gloom that always followed our uneasy breakfasts. Work was a barely tolerable distraction that evaporated into afternoons of restless daydreams and morbid gazing. Sallie, at least, still had the boozy dinners, just no longer with me. She would come home drunk, caustic. Nights descended into bitterness and silence: the unspoken conflict that defined the boundaries of our relationship. And the wilderness that lay beyond it.

When the taxi dropped me off a week ago, the cabin was almost obscured by the encroaching garden, now as dense and unkempt as the beard I'd let grow since Sallie left. I had taken the key from its hiding place beneath the deck, peeling back the wispy vortices of abandoned funnel webs. Inside, the air was stale and damp and had a faint tang that I later came to associate with rat droppings. The draining board was still stacked with plates and glasses from our last meal here, now sticky with dust. A half-drunk bottle of wine had turned to vinegar by the sink.

When I arrived that day, I did not yet know what compelled me or why I had come. The cabin held me in a kind of relentless gravity, drawing me toward some notion of completion that, however vague, was left unsatisfied by Sallie's parting. Perhaps I felt that something had been left behind here, some ghost of the person I had once been, or, perhaps, some essence of those happier times, that I might reabsorb by simple proximity. It's possible there were other reasons, but, if so, they were obscure. On some days, it felt as though I was here to say goodbye to Sallie, to finally let go of whatever it was we had shared and move on with my life. On others, I felt I was here to get closer to her, to connect with her once again through spaces she had once occupied and objects she had once handled, to rekindle an intimacy between us that existed now only in inanimate things, and in emptiness and silence.

Although I knew that I would not be disturbed as long as she was in Europe, I often fantasised about surprising Sallie here in some way. Returning home from her travels, seeking solitude in her old retreat. Or perhaps a romantic escape with some new man. These daydreams whiled away the long afternoons and left me with an unusual sense of calm and a feeling one might almost describe as joy.

How would she react to finding me here? I wondered. What strange shape might that encounter take?

#

The wound left by the leech continued to bleed for many hours after I returned. The thin fluid streamed from my calf so profusely that I ran through the cabin's entire supply of band-aids to staunch it, replacing them each time the blood soaked to the edges of the dressing.

It also began to itch: a maddening tingling sensation that gnawed away at me, no matter how I tried to distract myself from it.

Between the itching and the incessant changes of dressing,

that tiny puncture consumed my attention well into the afternoon. My mind came back again and again to the leech, the memory growing in vividness and intensity as I turned it over upon itself. And the more I dwelt on it, the more abstracted my deliberations became. Away from the rainforest, where every frond dripped with the threat of tangible parasites, my thoughts spiralled into a vortex of vague anxieties and phobic imagery. It was as though the heightened clarity of this memory was at the expense of a context that moored it in reality. Underlying everything, feeding and growing fat on my obsession, disgust was coiled inside me like an unnameable black thing, writhing in my belly, gagging in my throat, and pulling back the corners of my mouth into a grimace. At first, this nameless revulsion was directed at the leech. But as the colour drained from inside the cabin and the blue-grey dusk enveloped me, the feeling began to shift and I grew disgusted with myself.

On the one hand, my feelings toward the leech seemed completely justified, a primal horror that was only natural considering its grotesque otherness. It was repulsive. A hideous creeping parasite. An alien. A thief. Its very nature seemed an offence to warm-blooded creatures of every species. Its foul body: spineless and glistening. Its sickening gait: puppet-like and ludicrous. Its means of survival: stealthy, deceitful, insidious. Just picturing it made me boil with anger all over again.

And it was this anger that troubled me most of all, that kept me picking over the scene again and again, scratching at it and worrying it like the sore spot on my calf. How could I dare feel disgust at a creature simply for feeding on me, when my response had been to take its life? How much blood had the leech taken from me? And how much did I have to spare? Surely I could have shared that little bit of myself for the sake of a life?

The tension between these conflicting extremes bound me in an unresolvable, and quite intolerable, state of agitation that lasted well into the night. As I lay awake in the small bed that Sallie and I had once shared, I was overcome with pity for the leech and with remorse for what I had done to it. Like words of spite that erupted unbidden into one of my few arguments with Sallie, or the many times I let slip something about myself that did not hold with the image I had cultivated, I couldn't take this back, no matter how much I may have yearned to. I could not undo what I had done or return the leech to life. Knowing this, and finding no possible way to right it, was an agony that oppressed me like a storm that wouldn't break.

The rats that night were particularly bold. I had left a cupboard door open in the kitchen and I could hear their tiny feet skittering amongst the boxes of cereal and open packets of crackers. When I first arrived at the cabin, I had found a rat by the garden tap, the body of one at least, flat and completely desiccated. I knew the cabin was peppered with unsprung traps and boxes of poison, their lids peeled back to reveal the deadly green lollies inside. My heart had gone out to this poor creature, which, believing it to be food, had filled her belly with the poison. It must have taken days to parch her from within, sucking all the moisture from her body. She had died beside the dripping tap, no doubt in a desperate, doomed attempt to slake her undying thirst. Before unpacking the meagre supplies I'd brought with me, I had gone round to every corner of the cabin, every cupboard and cabinet, springing the traps and emptying the poison into the bin. As long as I was there, I wasn't going to be responsible for the death of an innocent creature. The rats had no less right to be in the cabin than I had.

The noise, along with my deliberations, kept me awake for many hours. Listening to the rats in the cupboard — gnawing on crackers, upending the open bags of rice — made me question still further my reaction to the leech. Why had my response been so extreme? What was the real root of my disgust? Where had the anger come from? And the violence? Why was I able to accept the rats, feeding themselves on the food that should have fed me, yet recoiled from the leech, following its instincts to precisely the same end?

These thoughts came from the shadowed border between sleep and wakefulness, folding over upon each other, collapsing together into a dreamlike soup of impressions and ideas that merged at last into a united vision. A vision that was at once transcendent and monstrous. It was as if a curtain had been pulled aside, revealing the inescapable perversity of nature: to be born hungry, a belly that lives only to feed itself, alive only at the expense of other lives. Purposeless and interminable, compelled to live, to feed, only to make meat to feed some other starving belly. The pointlessness and horror of it was overwhelming. The hunger never satisfied. The hunger unto death.

At the peak of the vision, I saw all life as nothing more

89

than a grotesque sculpture of mouths devouring mouths devouring mouths. A multitude, an infinity, expressed as a single mouth devouring a single meal.

And that meal was itself.

#

I must have slept, for I dreamed; long vivid dreams that I had no memory of on waking. Still, I felt them weighing on me like an old overcoat, heavy with melancholy and a nebulous longing. It had been raining while I slept and the cabin was ripe with the perfume of the rainforest. This fragrance intermingled with the funk of my forgotten dreams, as though, for want of sleep, I had become porous and was both absorbing the moisture of the rainforest and, at the same time, spilling out into it.

There was little breakfast to speak of. I rummaged in the kitchen for whatever scraps the rats might have overlooked, but all they had left was a scene of devastation and abandon. Rice was everywhere. Spilled from the upended bag, it was pooled in dry rivers on the Laminex work surface and sprayed across the kitchen floor like the dead husks of fallen stars. The cupboards themselves were bare of everything but crumbs, shredded boxes, and the ubiquitous peppering of dry turds. In the fridge, I found a small piece of cheese and the last apple. I tossed the cheese onto the deck for the possums and set out for my morning walk, eating the apple as I went.

The morning was oppressively humid, thick with moisture from the night's rain and already pregnant with the heat of the coming day. Even at this early hour, it was too hot for clothes, so I walked in nothing but my hiking boots and a pair of cut-off shorts. Unlike previous mornings, I had no plan, yet my feet seemed to know exactly where they were going.

I took the main track through the gates of the national park and down into the rainforest. Instead of turning up toward the lookouts, I continued to descend, leaving the path to follow the creek into the lushest nooks of the forest. I found a small pool beneath a terrace of lazy waterfalls, where the canopy above was so thick that no sunlight could penetrate. I settled down in the cool gloom and pulled off my boots, sat on the moist edge with my feet in the water.

It wasn't long before they found me there.

Before I even reached the pool, several leeches had already attached themselves. I wasn't sure exactly how many. I could see one on my calf and another further up my thigh, both of them quivering as they drew blood into their expanding bodies. At least one had settled on my back, but there may have been others. Knowing they were on me, seeing them feed, the feelings of disgust arose again. But, unlike the day before, I did not react. The emotions where still there, just detached somehow; only another tangled shape within that body, with its mouth and its belly, with its hunger and fear and other drives of a distinctly animal nature.

And more were converging. Other leeches inching through the foliage toward the bare white flesh, heads twitching on the end of undulant black stalks. They swivelled this way and that as if sniffing the air, sensing the promise of warmth and of nourishment. I felt the feather-light touches of tail suckers and mouths, the delicate end-over-end as the leeches made their ponderous climb, seeking out a space on which to attach. On which to feed.

I must have cut a strange sight as I returned from the park that lunchtime. The track was busier than usual and I encountered many other walkers before I reached the cabin. There were families, couples, and lone hikers like myself. Every one of them recoiled when they saw me approach, flattening themselves against the edge of the path to clear the way for me. One man was so disturbed he tripped over the snaking roots of a Watkin's Fig and almost fell backwards into the foliage. On his, and on every face, that same look. The flaring nose, the downward pull at the edge of the lips; the unmistakable grimace of disgust. They talked too, talked about me as I passed, as if I couldn't hear, as if I was in some way contrary to them. I heard one woman retch behind me.

I had to laugh. Hadn't my face been contorted by these same emotions only the day before? I felt for them. All they could see was the wild young man storming along the path, his eyes perhaps a little too wide, revealing a little too much white. They saw the expression, at once intense and serene, that encompassed a grin, uncomfortably twisted. They would have seen the body, bristling with the glistening black hairs that swelled and rippled and writhed as though with life of their own, pulsing shapes that dropped to the ground like rotten fruit, leaving thin ribbons of red to darken his shorts, streak his legs, and pool in the fluffy bands of his socks. I couldn't blame them for their feelings of horror and revulsion. They couldn't see beyond the mechanics. They lacked the vision.

Although it was all downhill, the final stretch to the cabin seemed endless. I must have given away a fair bit of blood by then, for I felt giddy and weak. Each step took considerable effort. When I finally reached the cabin, having left a breadcrumb trail of engorged leeches that led all the way back to the forest, I was so drained that I flopped straight into bed. I didn't even have the strength to pull my boots off.

#

I awoke later to the sound of rain drumming on tin. I had no idea what time it was. The light seemed to have leaked out of everything, creating an effect both shadowless and grey. It must have been evening, for I could hear the rats in the kitchen and could feel the pinch of cold on my skin. The bed was soaked.

I made to sit up, to put my legs out over the side of the bed, to stand, change out of my bloody shorts and into something warmer, perhaps scratch around in the kitchen for a bite. But I could barely sit up. Even that small movement made my head swim and I lay there, feeling the world flip-flop around me.

Then the itching began.

Not the uncomfortable irritation that I had felt the day before, but a seething anger in my arms and legs and chest. Had I been suspended from a thousand burning hooks and slowly pulled apart, it could not have been worse than this. I longed to scratch, but even that movement was too much to contemplate. My arms lay lifeless beside me on the blood-soaked sheets, as flaccid and impotent as the swollen bodies that still squirmed there.

I think I began to cry then, for my body convulsed and my eyes were shut so tight that my head ached. It's hard to contemplate now exactly why I wept: despair perhaps, or regret. It may have been simply the only means of escape from the pain, which swarmed beneath my skin like a colony of fire ants. Whatever the reason, those tears were cleansing. They didn't take the pain away, but they took me out of myself, out of my body. They allowed me to let go of everything. And in that letting go, I became weightless, unencumbered by the thoughts and feelings and memories that had bound me to myself. I felt as though I were floating upward, the itching and the weakness and the wetness now so dilute as to be almost imperceptible, completely overwhelmed by the greater flood of transcendence, of oneness, of interconnectedness with all things.

There must have been nothing left in the kitchen worth eating, for, sometime later, a rat came to visit me where I lay. Emboldened perhaps by my immobility, she hopped up onto the foot of the bed and perched on the toe of one of my walking boots. I watched her lift her head and sniff all around, teeth bared, nose twitching. The bed, I realised, must have smelled like a butcher's shop, of blood curdling as it dried, of meat that was just beginning to turn. She tiptoed down the ladder of laces and stopped at the bunched-up end of my sock, leaning out over my calf to take another sniff, not little sips this time but long questioning inhalations.

I barely felt the first bite. Watching her little jaw at work, tugging, first tentatively and then with incredible focus, at the ligaments of my lower calf, I experienced... nothing. A distant pulling sensation, like someone unthreading a bootlace.

Soon, other rats began to pop up over the sides of the bed. They didn't take long to tuck in. Before long, they covered my legs, tails curling, pulling off strips with those coarse yellow teeth. They were unstitching me, one red ribbon at a time. And by then, I was too weak to even lift my head, let alone to sit up and sweep them away.

And, I wondered, would I even want to? I had shared my blood. Should I not share my flesh as well?

I had always felt I had so much to offer, so much to give, but Sallie never saw it that way, how good I could have been for her. She saw only a vacuum, an emptiness that emptied her. Her loss. She would never understand. I can see that now. Not like my new friends with their simple needs, so easy for me to satisfy.

What would Sallie think if she could see me now?

I picture her, weeks, maybe months from today, returning to the cabin. The doors, once the threshold between the small but civilised inner space and the boundless incivility of wild nature, are now open wide. The smell of damp and decay is everywhere. Frogs, birds, lizards, and the legion tiny marsupials, have made their homes here, in the water pooling from the holes in the roof, in the branches that pierce the fly screens, amongst the rotting foam spilled from decrepit furniture, and in every one of the many boltholes and crawlspaces that now perforate the cabin. Fungi, moulds and grasses bloom throughout. Like the veins of a great living organism, tree roots have burst through the mock linoleum floor, vines have ripped through the ceiling. Twisting, coiling, interwoven, they lead Sallie to the living heart of the house, the bloody bedroom, and my parting gift. What will she think? How will she react to find, in that bed, which held us close so many nights, the hiking boots and the gleaming skeleton, so white against its flag of red, seething still, perhaps, with the life of a multitude. The centre of a living ecosystem.

What will she think of me then?

Inside the cabin, all is grey. It's as though all the colour has leeched from the room, and whatever world still exists outside of it. Even the crimson sheets are now just a deeper, darker shade of grey. It is neither night nor day, but a perpetual twilight, as though we are caught, my friends and I, hovering in a borderland between twinned worlds: light and dark, satiety and hunger, numbness and pain, life and the absence of life. It is as poignant as a dream. And I can't help but wonder if this greyness exists without — in the room, in the insatiable gnawing of the rats, in the droning of the flies, in the silent procession of the many ants — or whether this absence of colour, of contrast or tone, is in fact mine, dimming, faltering, fading unerringly to white.

I can hardly believe I have anything left to offer. Yet here we still are, all of us together, sharing this last meal. My true friends and I.

VERONICA'S DOGS
Cameron Trost

'You have often asked me about cases of species dysphoria, Charles.'

Charles Radic closed his copy of the Australian Journal of Psychology and dropped it onto his desk. He had been under the tutelage of Professor Broughton for nearly five years and knew when the University of Queensland's most highly regarded expert on psychosis was about to say something memorable.

'If I tell you a secret, will you promise to keep your lips sealed?'

Radic grinned. His tutor had a taste for the dramatic. 'Of course, I promise.'

Professor Broughton took a bottle of Lagavulin from the small cabinet beside his desk and poured two glasses before commencing.

'Last year, after several complaints from residents living near Bowman Park in Bardon, police arrested a man. He had been acting strangely and sleeping in the rushes along the banks of Ithaca Creek. More bizarrely still, he had been coming into the yards of homeowners who had dogs and eating from their bowls. One resident even caught him marking his territory.'

'You can't be serious?' Radic asked, the repugnant thought causing his brow to crease and his nose to flare up.

'But I am.'

'What became of him?'

'The authorities reacted intelligently for a change and a media circus was avoided. The man was given expert attention. I can vouch for that.'

Radic clasped his hands together in front of his mouth. This was the most intriguing tale Professor Broughton had ever shared with him, and that was saying a lot.

'It would be an exaggeration to claim that this chap is now of sound mind, or that he ever was or will be. But he has certainly returned to the human race, for whatever that is worth.'

'What a strange case!'

'It is indeed, and you don't know the half of it yet,' the professor continued as he took a few sheets of paper from the bottom drawer of his desk. 'Would you allow me to read his account of the incident that led to the onset of dysphoria to you?'

'I'm all ears,' Radic answered.

'These are the patient's words. He is very articulate and his honesty is admirable. This account will prove to be an invaluable aid in comprehending the mind of a dysphoric individual. I have, of course, changed his name so as to protect his identity, and in order to avoid placing your good self in a compromising position. For his part, he refused to reveal the identity of the woman involved despite the insistence of his therapists. Arguably, she is in even greater need of attention than he is.'

'Understood,' Radic said, although his choice of word was

clearly inappropriate given the context.

With that, Professor Broughton began.

#

This is my account of the events leading up to my psychotic episode. I have changed the names of the people involved and refuse to reveal their identities even to you, my therapist. After all, you are the one who has made me realise that nobody else is responsible for what happened to me. I should also point out that the wording of the exchanges reported in this account is not exact, but I have done my best to present the details of my experience as accurately as possible.

I first saw the woman I will call Veronica at a café in Bardon one Saturday morning after cycling with my friend and neighbour, Anders. We had stopped, as was our weekend ritual, for a flat white after a vigorous ride. I had never been to that particular café before, but I was to make the mistake of returning there on innumerable occasions over the following months.

While Anders was ordering our coffees at the counter, I noticed a dignified woman in an immaculate white and violet tracksuit sitting at a table by the door. What struck me about her at first was not her beauty, or the way her dark shoulder-length hair looked as though it had just been coiffed when it was obvious that she had been jogging, but the fact that her dog, a handsome and proud boxer, was sitting opposite her as though they were engaged in conversation.

My reaction was immediate and intense, one that I suppose

romantics would have classified as love at first sight. But I am no romantic, and I now know that this feeling was far more complicated and inexplicable than any classical *coup de foudre*. As it happened, her appearance and the fact that she was treating her pet like a person greatly aggravated me. Although I am no stranger to middle-class snobbery myself, it was her air of pretentiousness that annoyed me so much about this woman. Every perfectly placed hair and every drop of perspiration that she dabbed from her forehead with a violet handkerchief screamed arrogance and vanity. Then, before my very eyes, she poured two glasses of water and placed one in front of her canine companion.

It was ridiculous and incongruous. I found myself both despising and desiring this strange woman, and I have to admit, if I am to be completely honest with you, that I had an overriding urge to give her a good spanking right there in the café.

Little did I know at that confounding moment that another surprise was in store. On his way back from the counter, Anders stopped at her table and spoke to her. He patted the dog's head and I noticed her grimace, momentarily creasing her regal brow. Then, he pointed at me and I felt my whole body tighten as she stared straight into my eyes. I felt exposed.

A second later, she turned back to Anders and flashed him a fake smile.

It wasn't until my friend was sitting opposite me that I managed to tear my gaze away from the woman.

'Who's that?' I asked him as flatly as I could.

He told me her name and informed me that he had invited

her over for a drink that very evening. Anders' circle of friends was as wide as the Nullarbor Plain and it was unusual that I failed to make a new acquaintance whenever I attended one of his parties. Still a bachelor in my mid-thirties, Anders and his fiancée were accustomed to my need to flirt with any single woman amongst their friends, and I had, on several occasions, gone home with fellow partygoers.

'I can see she has caught your attention,' my friend whispered.

'Is it that obvious?'

Anders gave me a hard cold stare and then glanced quickly at Veronica.

'I regret inviting her now. I should have known better. She's an interesting girl and can be a lot of fun in small doses, but you don't want to get too close.'

'You know I like them quirky,' I reminded him.

'Listen, just trust me on this. I'm warning you,' he continued. 'Stay away from this one, mate. She's messed up. She's the kind of girl you can have a laugh with over a drink, but nothing more.'

It was clear by the stern tone of his voice and his stony expression that his words were to be taken seriously. But it was too late. I was infatuated.

For the first time since we had been friends, which was close to six years, I was angry at Anders. I was aware of how ludicrous it was, but his words had deeply offended me, as though he had spoken about a woman I had known intimately for years. I have never been married, and expect I never will be fit to take on such a commitment, but I imagined that a husband would react the same way to criticism aimed at his beloved wife.

I turned to look at Veronica and found her sipping at a cup of coffee and flicking through the morning newspaper. She stopped at one page and frowned. Then, she spun the paper around and showed it to her dog, raising her razor-thin eyebrows, silently asking her pet for his opinion of the article. It was so deliciously ridiculous of her and again an uncontrollable urge came over me.

Anders clicked his fingers at me and my head snapped back toward him. He flinched, half expecting me to lash out at him. His eyes widened and he shook his head.

'Don't do this, mate. Get a grip,' he whispered desperately. 'You don't want to go there.'

I closed my eyes and nodded, but I didn't mean it.

That night, at Anders' place, I wasn't myself. Or so he kept telling me. He told me to knock it off and have some fun, but I just kept asking him where Veronica was and by nine-thirty decided that my suspicions were true. He had surely called her and retracted the invitation.

'Tell me the truth, mate,' I said once I had drained yet another bottle of Byron Bay lager. 'You told her not to come, didn't you?'

'I did,' he admitted. 'Now, just forget about her. I wish I hadn't even spoken to her this morning. I should have known this would happen. You always do this.'

'What's that supposed to mean?' I hissed.

'You always go for the wrong types. That's what it means.

You'll never have a serious relationship if you keep doing that.'

'Wrong type? Maybe I'm a wrong type too!'

'No, you're not. You're my mate, and you're a good bloke. I don't want to lose you.'

'So, that's how it is!' I practically yelled. 'I have to choose, do I?'

A dozen faces turned to see what all the commotion was about.

'You don't have to choose, mate. I just want you to make the right decision.'

'Don't worry, I will!'

But I didn't. I stormed out of the house and have barely spoken a word to Anders since that evening. I hope, one day, to make contact with him again. I know he wants to remain my friend and help me recover, but I am so ashamed of myself.

After leaving the party, I walked from Anders' home in Ashgrove up to the hilltop suburb of Bardon. You have told me that Anders tried to find me that night, knowing where I had gone. He must have got behind the wheel despite being over the alcohol limit, but I didn't see his silver Land Rover. The poor fellow, I've put him through so much. I will apologise to him one day, once I can bring myself to do it properly.

In Bardon, I crept into people's gardens and peered through lit windows. The suburb is a vast one and the notion that I could be so lucky as to stumble upon Veronica simply by sneaking around like some kind of pervert was absolutely ridiculous. However, I was barely aware that I no longer belonged to the world of the sane. I reassured myself that anybody who felt love or lust for another was beyond sanity, and that I wasn't alone.

Needless to say, my foray was unsuccessful. I came close to being caught by one woman who heard her verandah floorboards creak as I approached a window. The front door lock turned before I had time to stumble down the steps that separated the verandah from the garden path, but I could just make out a man's voice telling her that it was only possums and not to be so paranoid all the time. She must have accepted his advice because the door remained closed.

In another yard, facing Ithaca Creek, I came close to being mauled by a German shepherd. I had jumped a fence after noticing a woman who might have been Veronica washing dishes at a side window. The dog barked once and then came racing out of nowhere. It was almost on top of me before I had even caught sight of it. I was terrified and thought that my time had come. But for some reason — and looking back, this was the first sign of my dysphoria — when the animal growled at me, my instinct was to take a step toward it and growl right back at it. Indeed, I think I roared. The dog came to a halt within striking distance of my face, cocked its head in confusion, and then actually started backing away. I did the same, backing slowly away until I reached the front gate and could make a hasty departure.

My recollection of what happened then is unclear, but I must have decided to go home, because I woke up in bed the next morning. I was still fully dressed and my clothes were covered in leaves, prickles, and dirt. My legs ached terribly.

My muscles were used to cycling long distances, but not to walking, crawling, and jumping.

I took a quick shower and decided to drive, not ride, to the café in Bardon, hoping against all hope that Veronica would be there and that I would know what to say to her. But she wasn't, and after almost two hours and too many flat whites, I went home heartbroken.

I returned to the café on Monday morning, on the way to work, but Veronica wasn't there. I tried again on Tuesday morning, but the result was the same. I decided instead to cycle the streets of Bardon every evening that week, searching for a dark-haired princess with a boxer. I was pathetic, I was miserable, and I was unsuccessful.

Then, on Saturday morning, the first I hadn't spent with Anders in a long time, I rode to the café.

No sooner had I arrived at the door than I saw Veronica, dressed in a red tracksuit and gingerly dipping a jam drop into her mug of coffee. Her hair was perfect, shining in the warm morning sunlight that flooded through the doorway as though directing customers toward the counter. The boxer was sitting opposite, his posture as elegant as that of his owner, and he wore a studded collar that was the exact same shade of red as Veronica's tracksuit. It was all absurdly gorgeous.

I was simultaneously enthralled and aggravated by her all over again. I felt my knees buckle. She had weakened them. She had done what some of the toughest cycle paths in the state had been unable to do. I was like putty, but I didn't know whether she would want me in her hands.

She recognised me and twitched the corners of her lips. It wasn't exactly a smile, but it wasn't a frown either. The boxer looked at me too, with complete disinterest, the way he might watch a leaf fall from a tree.

I gathered up enough courage to speak to her. 'Hello,' I said. 'You didn't come to Anders' party last week.'

She seemed surprised. 'He told me there was a problem and he'd had to cancel it!'

'Oh, did he?' I said, shaking my head.

'What a dick!' she hissed, yet she managed to make those crude words sound quite classy.

'Can I buy you a coffee?'

'Thank you. That's very kind. But no,' she answered. 'I'm here with Bruce.'

She must have noticed that I was shocked, because she practically scowled at me. What kind of excuse was that for not accepting an offer? And what kind of a name for a dog was Bruce? I wanted to slap her square across her pretty face. I wanted to chain bloody Bruce to an awning post outside the café and have my way with the princess right there in front of him. I wanted to teach her not to be so weird and annoying, and to teach her dog not to sit on chairs in cafés.

'Are you sure?' I asked her, trying hard to remain civil.

'Yes, it was nice meeting you. You seem like a decent person... for a cyclist.'

Fuming, I turned around and left the café before I ended up doing something I would regret.

I rode around the block several times, and when I saw her leave, I followed her home.

You can't begin to imagine how relieved I was to see that she had Bruce on a lead, although the fact that it was the exact same shade of red as his collar and her tracksuit made it look more like a fashion accessory than a means of control. Bruce walked by her side, not in front or behind, and didn't stop to sniff at the base of power poles or trees. He trotted along with the same air of calm self-satisfaction as his owner.

Veronica's posture was perfect. Her hair swung from side to side like a pendulum and the tight mounds of her buttocks bobbed up and down hypnotically with every step she took. Her pace was so quick that I was able to follow quite comfortably on my bicycle without losing balance.

I won't give details of the location, but when she arrived at her house, I watched from behind a tree as she jogged up the front stairs and onto the verandah. She unleashed the dog and slipped her red trainers off before reaching into the pocket of her hoodie and removing the keys to the house. She unlocked three doors. The first was a wrought iron grill, the second a security door with a fly screen, and the third a solid wooden door. She was obviously an anxious woman, locking three doors just to go for a jog and a coffee, and that provoked an even stronger desire in me to continue pursuing her. It wasn't the dog she needed to keep her safe and sound. It was me. She needed me to make sure she didn't fall victim to a rapist or a pervert.

I know what you are thinking, and you are quite right, of course. However, at that point in time, the irony of my situation was lost on me. I failed to realise that stalking a woman was not normal behaviour for a man who had always considered himself both law-abiding and of sound mind. Likewise, the cognitive dissonance — a term you have taught me — of fantasising about protecting a woman while feeling a barely controllable urge to take her by force failed to dawn on me until recent weeks.

Once Veronica and her dog had gone inside, I heard a low whimper and found myself looking behind me, half expecting to find a stray puppy. Of course, there was nothing and nobody. I was alone in the street.

My bladder was full, so I urinated against the tree, and then I got back on my bike and rode home.

My intention had been to resist the urge to go back to Veronica. But I couldn't. The thought of going to bed without catching another glimpse of her filled me with a kind of heavy emptiness.

As the sun sank behind Mount Coot-tha, I rode back to Bardon. It was already dark when I arrived in her street and hid my bike behind the tree I had used as cover earlier that day. The air was cool and dark clouds threatened to empty their load on me, but I remained undeterred. I sniffed at the air and was convinced I could smell her delicious perfume, the one that she wore jogging for whatever reason. Of course, it must have been a figment of my increasingly incongruous imagination.

I was wearing my black cycling shorts and jersey so that I wouldn't be easily spotted in the dark as I entered Veronica's garden and crept up to her house.

There was a light on around the back, but the house was up

on stumps, and although there was a deck, there was no exterior staircase leading up to it.

I was going to have to climb.

After glancing up at the neighbour's house to make sure that I wasn't being observed, I clambered up one of the steel posts that supported the deck and climbed over the railing. Making a quick escape wouldn't be easy, but I somehow hoped that if Veronica did catch me, she would be so kind as to invite me inside. A woman living by herself must get lonely sometimes and need a little company.

Stepping over to the window, being careful not to bump into the deck chair or empty washing basket and making sure I stayed out of the light, I soon learned that I was wrong. She wasn't lonely at all. Veronica and Bruce were sitting on the couch, watching television together. They had their backs to me, and if it hadn't been for the window, I would have been able to smell her hair.

The boxer's ears twitched for a moment and my muscles froze in response. But it didn't turn around or start barking.

Veronica seemed to be eating dinner, judging by the way she raised her right arm with her elbow pointing out every few seconds. Then, she did something that disgusted me, and I almost made the mistake of gasping. She offered some of her food to Bruce and let him eat it from the fork. He licked it off and I screwed my face up as I noticed his slobber sticking to the fork once she had pulled it away.

She then ate another mouthful.

My disgust soon changed to indignation. An elegant woman like her had no right to behave in such a disgraceful way. She was breaking the rules of basic human decency. Letting her dog sit next to her on the couch while she ate dinner was one thing, but sharing her meal and her fork with him — no, *it* — was outrageous.

I felt like slapping her, and I felt like giving Bruce a hiding. She needed me there beside her, not some filthy mongrel.

I heard a growl. Then, an instant later, Bruce spun around. He snarled at me through the window and gave a warning growl.

By the time he had started barking, I was off the deck and sprinting back toward my bicycle. I had no idea whether Veronica had seen me.

It wasn't until I was on two wheels and speeding away that the realisation struck me that the first growl I had heard had been different from the second.

That was the first of many nights spent peering into Veronica's house. Each time I rode up to Bardon, I knew that I was sinking deeper into a pit of obsession and anguish from which it would be difficult to climb back out, as indeed it has been and continues to be. Nevertheless, Veronica was under my skin. I pitied and despised and craved this strange and vulnerable woman. I was convinced that she needed me. She was lonely and afraid. That's why she was so close to her dog. The animal offered her the companionship and sense of security that a single woman needed, but it wasn't how she ought to live. I had to show her that it was me she needed.

Before long, I started sleeping in the park opposite her

house and stopped going to work. My memory of this time is unclear, but the more I watched her, the more I wanted her and the more I hated Bruce. I was bitterly jealous of the dog. I became very adept at creeping around in the dark and quickly learned how to avoid being detected. It all came down to paying attention to the direction of the wind, so as to avoid him catching my scent, and to moving in complete silence.

I had suppressed the last night I watched Veronica from my memory until you dug it up. Of course, I am glad you did. Otherwise, I would still be roaming the streets like a lost dog and thinking about her. Now, I am becoming human again.

It was raining heavily that night but I was impervious to the wet and cold as I crawled out from the reeds growing by the bank of Ithaca Creek and shuffled over to Veronica's house. I forced myself to ignore the bolts of lightning that struck nearby and the crashes of thunder that boomed across the turbulent sky. I steadied my legs and carried on.

I had fallen into the habit of climbing a jacaranda tree that allowed me a very narrow view of Veronica in the shower. Sometimes, Bruce was in there with her, even though it seemed to be against his will, judging by the way she held him firmly by the collar with one hand while she scrubbed at his body with the other. Naturally, I preferred it when she was alone, but whenever Bruce was with her, I took great pleasure in admiring the way her breasts jiggled as she energetically rubbed soap into his coat.

But that night, the bathroom light was off. I had evidently missed the show.

There was purple light, not unlike the colour of jacaranda flowers, coming from the room one window down, so I moved a little further along the branch, well aware that I was increasing my chances of slipping, losing my balance, having the branch snap under my weight, or even being struck by lightning. None of that mattered to me at all. I simply had to see her.

The room's white lace curtains were almost closed and rain was hammering against the window panes, but every now and then, I managed to catch a glimpse of movement. The gap between the curtains exposed the purple lamp whose light fell upon a flat floral patterned surface behind it.

I realised with delight that I was peering, for the very first time, into Veronica's bedroom.

A flash of lightning lit the sky for a moment and the corresponding boom of thunder made the branch I was perched upon shake. Undeterred, I ventured a little further along, grasping the rough, wet surface as firmly as I could.

The movements I had noticed were ever so slightly clearer now.

After another minute of observation, I noticed that they were rhythmic, like dancing. A moment later, I was able to distinguish a heavenly glimpse of Veronica's white skin through the rain-spattered window. I started breathing heavily, and despite my discomfort, my penis went hard and bulged against the jacaranda branch. There was no doubt about it. She was masturbating. As I watched, I found myself rubbing against the tree in time with her.

After a while, her body arched and she shifted a little

toward the head of her bed. It was then that I caught sight of what was on the bed with her.

I felt sick to the core as I realised what was happening. It was disgusting and inhuman. But my shock was cut short by a fork of lightning that ripped through the dark clouds and struck nearby. The last thing I can remember before coming into your care is falling from the branch and hitting the ground as a thunderclap rattled my bones.

#

Professor Broughton poured another dram of whisky into each glass.

'Remember, Charles, that you promised to keep your lips sealed.'

Charles Radic simply stared at his tutor with an expression of horror and disbelief.

'Are you all right?'

'Yes,' he whispered. 'Well, I suppose so. Tell me, it is true? You're surely playing a joke on me. It's too bizarre to have actually happened.'

Professor Broughton shook his head. 'I'm afraid it's all too real, Charles. Truth is stranger than fiction and all that, right? Now, do remember, you mustn't repeat it to anybody. Your lips are sealed.'

'Repeat it!' Charles said, frowning. 'I don't even want to think about it ever again.'

BULLETS
Joanne Anderton

It had once been a sheep, and it wasn't dead yet. A mangle of smouldering wool, scorched skin, and cooked meat, breathing in puffs of hot ash. Outrun by flames, tangled in underbrush, or crushed beneath a falling tree, who could tell? Everything was charcoal now.

I pull the mask from my nose and mouth and breathe the warm smoke in. Load the rifle, aim between what's left of the poor thing's ear and eye, and give it peace with the slow squeeze of the trigger. Try to ignore the shakes, the tears stinging my eyes. I'm soaked in sweat and covered in ash, but supposed to be grateful that I'm still alive. At this point, it's hard to even give a shit that the house is still standing.

Thank God, mum. We thought you were a gorner this time.

Yeah, real fucking lucky.

This is not the way it was meant to be. Killing stock on my own with the sky still red.

Something rustles in the ash, the distinctive kick of dying feet and the moan of a painful breath. I pull the mask up and head for the sound. It's hard to breathe through the surgical cloth but it eases the coughing at the end of the day. Winding my way through split, black gumtrees and simmering hubs of still glowing embers, I dig in my bag for more bullets. It's difficult with the thick gloves on, my fingers slip and pinch through empty cardboard boxes.

The ground is uneven. I trip on a crumbling stump, clutch at a fragile branch that cracks in my grip, and almost fall on top of them.

A whole bloody herd.

'Shit.'

They're clustered together, so close in places I can't tell one corpse from the other. Ten of them, maybe more. Even with their sleek fur all charred and their long manes burnt away, there's a wildness about them that tells me these aren't my horses. They lie in a way that makes them look like they're still running. Legs bent and heads tossed back. Free things. Brumbies.

'Shit.' What else is there to say?

Then one of them moves. It kicks at the ash with blackened hooves, it breathes and it whinnies and I'm running over to it, jumping the bodies of its brothers and sisters in my haste. Poor thing can't still be alive. Its skin is hard and cracked like stone, but still its great barrel of a chest rises and falls in fast, jittery motions. Its lips are shrivelled back to reveal great white teeth that clench and clack.

'I'm so sorry.' I scramble for bullets but all I find are empty boxes. 'Shit!' Nothing. My bag is empty, my gun too. I'm standing here watching this beautiful creature die slowly, painfully, and I've run out of fucking bullets?

Its breathing is violent now, all four legs spasming, neck shaking. I take an unsteady step back, whispering pathetic apologies under my breath.

Then the creature splits in half, cleanly down the middle.

And a naked young man falls out.

#

His skin is piebald, his eyes are blue, his hair is long and always tangled with burrs no matter how often I brush it out. He is very strong and eager to please. Sometimes, he is too hot to touch. If he holds a piece of paper too long, it will catch on fire, but he doesn't get burned. The flames just dance on the white and grey patterns across his palm.

I gave him water to drink when I first got him home, and wiped the ash from his body with a damp cloth. He steamed, the scent reminding me of my husband on a hot day, and the stables on a humid night, human and animal, flesh and grass both.

For a long time, I just stared at him. He stood tireless in my kitchen, naked and silent. Watching me in turn. But I couldn't stand there doing nothing for ever, and as soon as I moved, he followed.

He doesn't speak, at least not that I have heard. But I'm accustomed to silence.

Why don't you sell up and buy a place in town? You must be lonely. And we worry about you, mum, all alone out there. Something could happen to you, and no one would know.

I've never felt alone out here. Not even after Mark died.

It started with the fence around the house. Thing was a mangled wreck from the flames, posts gone, wire tangled and useless. Just goes to show how close the fire came. He watched me dragging wood for new posts, straightening coils of wire from the shed. It was odd, I won't deny that, to be hammering posts into the earth with a naked man by my side, focused on my every move. But not as odd as leaving a fence unmended. Only took two, maybe three, before he seized the sledgehammer from me and set to work. He didn't so much as pause for a breath until the fence was complete.

The pale patches on his skin don't burn in the sun. He does start spot fires though, around his feet, if I'm not careful.

After the fence, he just turned to me, expectant. It was nearly night by then, so I led him back inside. Gave him more water. Vegemite sandwiches. I fished out some of Mark's old clothes from the boxes I keep them in...

It's not healthy, mum. They're just collecting dust. You've got to start letting go.

...but quickly worked out clothes weren't a good idea on him. Wasn't wearing them an hour before they started to smoke.

He's good at the manual stuff, the things Mark used to do. The chopping and the digging and the lifting. He reminds me of my husband sometimes, more than I'd like to admit, in his silence, his maleness, the strength of his youthful body. I remember muscles like those, the way they felt beneath my hands, his warmth a furnace against me.

Together, we emptied the shed so he could sleep on the cool cement floor. Every evening, I comb the burrs from his hair. Every morning, they've returned.

#

I lock him in the shed as a plume of dust heralds the arrival of

117

an ancient, battered ute. The bloke that steps down from the vehicle is just as ancient with a stooped back, wiry frame, and leather skin. Old Jimmy, my closest neighbour and a good twenty-minute drive away. He leans back with an audible crack, tips the notched edge of his lanky, grey Akubra, and says, 'You were lucky, missy.'

No matter how old I get, this man will always call me missy. Doesn't matter that I was married for forty years before Mark's death, either.

'The Collins family lost the house, but they were evacuated, so at least no one got hurt.' He inspects the damage even as he rambles. Usually, I'm expected to bring tea and some kind of cake when he appears. It's the way things are done. This time, I just watch him shuffle. 'Way too much stock lost, that's the real problem.' He's taking in the mended fence, the cleared firebreak, the larger trees chopped and stacked in neat piles, and I know he's wondering how this little missy who'd come to this place as a young and silly thing in love, and who'd never worked a farm before in her life could have done so much clearing up in only a couple of days.

'I know,' I say. 'I had to shoot a lot of sheep. I ran out of bullets.' It's a long drive into town to replenish them too.

He mumbles something about head of cattle, and acts of God, but I don't listen. I don't like the way he keeps using the word *luck*. He thinks I got off easy. He doesn't think that's fair.

When he finally leaves, I wait for the dust to settle completely before I unlock the shed.

He steps out into the sun and sniffs the air like an animal. I wonder what he makes of the lingering scent of old tobacco and cracked leather. He seems distracted all afternoon, even restless as I brush his hair. His fingers beat a quick tattoo on my bare knee. I wonder if he didn't appreciate being locked in the shed, or if he didn't like the presence of another man.

But then she steps out of the smoke-haze of the dim, twilight bush.

She is not piebald, and she is not large and strong. She is short, and timid, her skin an even olive tone, eyes wide and darting. She leaves tiny grass fires in her wake.

If he was a brumby before the fire, then I can only think she must have been a wallaby.

She's good with her hands. The shed with the generator was knocked out early on, damaged but not razed. It only takes a moment of my tinkering for her to get the idea. Sooner than I could believe possible, she's up to her elbows in machinery. Two days later, and the lights are on. I don't even know where she got the parts.

Wallaby is only the beginning.

They come as a trickle at first, and usually in the twilight, when the remnant smoke obscures their passage and the world is both day and night. I open the shed to them all, and their heat, their dripping flame. My wild horse moves into the house. He sleeps on the ensuite tiles, right by my bedroom door.

Short stocky wombat digs a new vegetable patch, while skinny lamb helps lay irrigation. My wild horse and a thickly set bull drag what's left of the pump out of the dam, which wallaby immediately sets to repairing. An emu girl with long legs, long arms, and sharp eyes rebuilds my clothesline.

I follow them around with the kitchen fire extinguisher and

wet towels. I plant the first seedlings myself, with my own cool fingers, and fertilise them with ash.

#

The first new fire starts a fortnight after the big one. Takes out a stockyard on the large station on the other side of town, and a poor penned-in flock unable to escape. It's small, because there's not much left to burn, so I suppose you have to be thankful for that.

'Thing is,' the old Jimmy drawls, as he sips his tea and takes in my quickly growing veggie patch with ogling eyes. 'They reckon it was deliberately lit.'

I suck a sharp breath. 'Who could be so stupid?' He's not allowed inside the house, where my brumby waits perched on the edge of the bathtub for him to leave.

'Dunno if I agree,' he says. 'Electrical storm that night, could as easily been that. No rain, lightning strike. Not the first one I've seen.' He gazes with longing at the empty table. The tea's weak and there's no cake.

'I have to go into town,' I say.

'Been too busy to do any baking, I imagine.'

I don't answer. I will have to go soon. My pantry is bare, the children who shuffle restless and sparking inside the locked shed are getting hungry. But I dread the thought.

How can I leave him?

That afternoon, five sheep women appear at the fence. They shiver and flame and mew, not taking to the garden or the chores. All they do is huddle in a tight fearful knot. I set up

120

sprinklers at their feet to douse the flames, because they will not be coaxed into the shed.

Maybe it is their sounds that wake me. I drag myself from my light sheets. The fan beats a regular drum above my head, slow and peaceful like imaginary rain. A few bleary steps to the window, and I look out.

My fire children aren't sleeping on the cool cement like I expected. Instead, they surround the shivering sheep women, and seem to be assessing them. A tight ring of scrutiny and fizzling fire. Don't know what they're looking for, or what decides them, but the decision is palpable. The sheep can't stay. Slowly, like a fiery tide, the children push the sheep out of the yard. There is no violence in the action, just pressure. The sheep women trip and stumble back. They bleat and beg, but are ignored.

'What...' I reach a hand out the open window, open my mouth to call them. What are they doing?

Then he is there. He places a damp hand on my arm. He's dripping water from the tap. It's already starting to steam, but for now, he is cool enough to touch. He wraps strong arms around my shoulders, soaking my nightie until it clings to my flushed skin. I can't help myself, and lean back against him. He smells like horse and man.

The sheep are pushed over the fence and out into the bush. The others glance at the house, for only an instant, before following.

My wild horse turns me away from the window and takes me back to bed. He lies me down and rests beside me, his face so close to mine, arm draped across my chest. I realise he's run himself a bath of cold water, and he rises from the bed to dip his body into it, so the mattress does not catch alight. I lie between the cool wet sheets and the hot weight of his body and call him Mark, because I do not know his true name.

The next morning, there are tiny singes on the sheets, small and round like cigarette burns. The children are up and already making repairs with the first light, and there is no hint that the sheep were ever here.

#

You okay, mum? Haven't heard from you in ages. Give us a call when you get this, won't you?

Love you.

Today, I have to go into town. I haven't had a proper meal in two days, and there's no fucking toilet paper. It's the loo paper that clinches it, really. There are just some things you can't go without.

I put a stop to work on an array of solar panels that are springing up on my roof, so I can lock the fire children in the shed. Everyone. Even him. It's a bit of a squeeze. Two calves and a whole clutch of rabbits have arrived over the past few days. Most of them sit with their knees drawn up, silent eyes resentful as I close the door. My wild horse just stands, in the centre, and watches me.

Takes three goes to start the car. The drive to town through ruined roads and blackened bush is surreal. I almost lose my way twice. Nothing looks the same. It's quiet in town. Seems the fire spread this far, further than I'd realised. Two houses on

122

the edge flattened. A general heaviness in the air that has nothing to do with smoke. There are fewer cars parked on the curb, fewer people drinking out the front of the pub. I tug my hat down low, shake my sleeves loose so they cover my arms, nod to old Jimmy with a VB in his hand, and head into the IGA.

Air con hits me like a fist in the chest. Awful stuff. I gather as fast I can. Toilet paper. White bread. Vegemite.

'Judy?'

Damn it.

'It is! Judy, thank goodness.'

I turn and paste on the smile.

Karen runs the supply and antiques. She sells farm equipment, old and new. The shiny and useful stuff that come with warrantees, and the rusty things teetering between valuable collectible and useless junk.

'G'day.' I shift my grip on the basket. Her eyes are taking everything in, from the mud on my boots to the five jars of vegemite and the small tower of bread. 'How'd you fare, Karen?'

She nods. Short cropped hair grey at the roots, flowers on her shirt, long nails painted red. 'Did okay, did okay. Got to the backyard fence but didn't get much further. Others ain't so lucky.' A pause. 'You?'

'House still standing,' I say.

'Better than that!' she says, and my stomach drops. Here it comes. 'Heard you were doing much better than that! Jimmy says the place is looking spic and span, like back when Mark was alive.'

123

I knew the old bastard had been gossiping. They always do.

'Who've you got working for you?' Young Anthony, with his two scrawny girls loitering at his feet, reaches past me to grab the milk. Doesn't meet my eye. His lips are pressed into a sour line. 'If you found some good help, you should send them round. Share the love, Judy.'

I mumble something and push on, not really paying much attention to what I throw into the basket now. It's always the way. Doesn't matter how remote you are or how small a thing, these people will know about it.

But Karen can't leave well enough alone. 'Not everyone's so lucky,' she says. Doesn't seem to be actually buying anything, just buzzing like a fly around my head. 'There's been more fires, you know? Not out where you are, but closer to town. Every couple of nights, one flares up. Can't tell where it will hit. No rhyme or reason. The Davidsons lost a silo. The Marsons' shearing shed went up in a blaze. People are scared, Judy.'

I remember what Jimmy said about lightning strikes. 'Deliberately lit?' I ask.

'Not everyone's got time to be planting lettuce, you know. Cops have even been called.'

The girl on the register is young, surly, and pierced. She won't stay round this place for long. When I hand her the money, she notices the burns on my wrist.

'Shit,' she hisses. 'Did you get caught in the fire?'

I shake my arm so the sleeves cover them. 'I'm fine.'

The burns were an accident, of course. My brumby can't

help the fire within him, and no amount of water will keep him cool for long.

'Think you should see a doctor for that,' the girl says, as she dumps coins into my hands.

'She'll be right.' I try another smile. Not sure it works.

Karen follows me to the car. 'You sure, Judy?' No longer a busybody, she actually sounds like she cares. I remember the bad days, years ago, when it looked like the drought would never let up. Her son-in-law — what was his name again? — hanged himself when they couldn't pay the bills. I held her hand but she wouldn't cry.

Mark refused to go to the funeral. He just muttered darkly, about people who were too weak to live on the land, and drank too much. Some nights, I'd have to lock myself in the bathroom.

Country women are supposed to stick together. If we don't look after each other, who will?

But I can't tell her about my brumby, can I?

'Of course, I am.' I throw the groceries in the boot. 'Been doing this on my own for long enough. I know what I can take.'

She nods, and her face is pinched and squinting. 'Just be careful, out there. On your own.'

We worry about you, mum. Out there all on your own.

I hesitate. 'Actually,' I say, as she turns to go. 'There is something you could do for me.'

A smile.

'Could you open the shop for a moment? I'm out of bullets.'

I arrive home in the twilight, and the shed door is wide open. My children wait by the side of the road, features hidden in shadow and eyes reflecting the glow of the headlights. They escort me through the gate, back to the carport. Isolated spot fires crackle in the lawn.

I make them sandwiches all night, because I can't bring myself to sleep.

#

I wake to the smell of smoke in the distance, the smudge of red on the horizon. His weight on me is hot and comforting but crushing the air from my lungs, both at once. I try to move but he holds my arms and kisses my face and it burns, but I kiss him back.

'Mark,' I call him, as the smoke wafts in through the open window.

It's just not safe anymore! We have a granny flat out back. It's quiet here. You won't even hear the traffic. Kate'll come pick you up. Please, mum, won't you think about it?

At dawn, the fire children return, climbing the fence, not even trying to hide. They've brought more with them — black cockatoos with red coloured streaks in their long dark hair. They screech and they scream as they tear down the old gums in the back paddock, bare hands stronger than chainsaw or axe.

Every night, before he takes me to bed, I watch them climb the fence and leave. Every morning, the scent of smoke carries the promise of death in it, and loss, as they return.

Cops come to the door and I can barely face them. No way

there'd be an arsonist round here. Fire's not a toy round here.

'Worst season we've ever seen.' The older of the two looks grave, serious. 'Freak grassfire got out of control last night, took out the caravan park. You know the one by the river, just outta town? Killed an old lady, pensioner, all on her own.' He glances around. 'You best be careful too.'

'Nice place you've got, missus.' The young cop, hardly a man, shields his eyes with the flat of his hand as surveys the garden, the new water tank, the solar panels, the extension out back. 'Can't imagine you looking after it all by yourself.'

The cops don't see the children, hidden in the shadows of the still blackened bush, eyes like embers.

They bleed out into the sunlight as the cops leave. Standing on the verandah, I survey them all. 'That's enough,' I whisper, and the bush is silent. 'You have to go.'

The fire children stare at me with no indication that they have understood.

'You have to stop doing this! Stop working here. I don't need you anymore. Stop lighting fires. You're hurting people. We're done. That's enough. Thank you. Now go.'

They pay me no mind, and return to work.

His hands on my arms are hot and dry. They burn right through to the skin. 'Tell them they have to go!' I cry as he turns me around and guides me inside.

He holds me, because it is what I need of him. The children fill my yard and clutter the house and work hard, and it has not been this way for so many years. But as I lie beneath his weight and smell smoke, I cannot help but think of the price.

127

#

I draw the rifle from its locked case, and gather my replenished ammunition. I pull on my gloves and my boots, tuck the mask in my pocket, take water and a vegemite sandwich. This is the way I have always done it, for many summers. At first, with Mark, who first taught me how to shoot. And recently, all alone.

The fire children do not seem to notice me leave, do not so much as pause in their work. The rabbits have started making an in-ground pool.

Enough is enough.

Only my wild horse watches, from the bedroom window, as I set out. I do not look back.

Their bodies are not as hard to find as I suspected. Perhaps that's the way it works, perhaps they need to be close.

The cockatoos are little more than puffs of ash and feathers, twitching with weakened breaths. Almost seems a pity to waste a bullet on them. The rabbits weren't wild. They were white and fat and obviously someone's precious pets, back legs kicking feebly. One by one, I put them out of their misery. Wallaby. Wombat. Emu. Cattle. Goat. A couple of dogs, a single cat. Even a lizard or two. Bullet between the eyes and ears, quick, clean, honed from years of practice.

Finally, I return to the brumby herd.

It's not safe there, all alone. Aren't you lonely, mum? Aren't you just a little bit scared?

I was never lonely out here.

128

When I return, the house is empty and quiet again. I lie on sheets still faintly damp and cradle the single remaining bullet in my hand.

SAVIOUR
Mark McAuliffe

By late afternoon, Neil was beginning to feel the burn. After an early dinner from the nearby takeaway, all he wanted to do was sit back, have a beer, just relax and watch the cricket highlights. Shit, it was his holiday too, wasn't it?

'He's late,' Kim said.

'Call him.'

'I did. Must have it switched off.'

'Yeah, well... don't worry about it. He'll be fine.'

'I told him to be back by five. It's already fifteen minutes after.'

'So?'

'So... he's late.'

He wasn't going to win. Seventeen years of marriage had taught him that. A few minutes later, he was pushing himself out of his chair.

'All right. All right! Enough!'

He went back to the beach. There was a lot less people there since he'd left just over an hour ago, and those who had braved it up until now were starting to shake out their towels, pack up their gear. No wonder, the storm clouds were rolling in fast from the far horizon. The weather report did say it could be a big one.

Maybe she was right to be worried.

Not that he'd ever admit it to her.

His light polyester shirt felt like hell against his sunburnt skin. His tender thighs forced him to walk bow-legged, made him look like a bloody idiot. He knew where Paul would be, over by Atlantis, at the northern end. A long frigging walk.

Little shit, more trouble than he's worth.

An unworthy thought and he immediately regretted it. He was in a bad mood, that was all, brought on by his annoyance by their choice for a holiday destination this year.

At first, it had seemed a good idea. Money had been a bit tight recently, what with the new car and rising school fees, so when that telemarketer had called with an offer of great deals at the new resort on the Gold Coast, they'd jumped at the chance. The perfect solution. Sorted.

Yet he had started to regret the decision from the moment he'd arrived. To be honest, he'd had a few misgivings before then, but, what with such enthusiasm from the wife and kids, how could he say no?

Millennium Beach. He even hated the name, thought up by slick salespeople to inspire hope for a more caring future. So futile. A complete holiday community, built from scratch upon the ruins of past human stupidity. An attempt to shore up the thin scrap of all that was left of a coast claimed by rising tides, not to mention recoup the enormous losses to the tourism industry these last few decades.

No expense spared in either the construction or the advertising; all those flashy prime time commercials announcing a new cooperative between the state government and big business.

That slogan: Come and see what you could have missed!

What idiot came up with that one? And what kind of dickheads did it take to give it the final nod of approval?

An enormous feat of engineering, he had to give them that. A whole new moulded shoreline. Imported sand. New species of plants, grown in a lab. Dunes sculpted by dozers, placed strategically to specific instructions, built just right. Shops and resorts laid with plans tried and tested in the United States and Europe, fitted together like one massive jigsaw.

Everything the same. Everything so damn neat.

Neil spat like he had a bad taste in his mouth. He was breathing heavier as he got closer to Atlantis. Up ahead he could just make out a couple of figures overlooking the choppy ocean. Another minute and he could recognise his son, crouching on the very edge of the retaining wall. The sight made his fists clench, unconsciously.

'Paul,' he hollered, 'get back from there!'

The boy turned his head to look in his father's direction. Neil was now close enough to notice the dreamy expression; the same slack look he wore whenever he contemplated those submerged ruins that began only metres from the shore. That was another thing that bothered Neil. Ever since they'd arrived a few days ago, and Paul had learned what was out there, it had held a deep fascination for him.

Atlantis. The lost city. More like a lost coastal suburb. But why quibble? It was an apt name, though certainly not the only place along the eastern Australian coast with such a title these days. And, of course, it wasn't a name endorsed in any of the glossy brochures. It was only late last year when the government had prevented that company from conducting tours. Safety fears they said, but everyone knew the real reason. Made the front pages for a while, much to the premier's chagrin.

'Get back from there, I said!'

On the second try, Paul's eyes snapped back into focus and he scuttled back. Satisfied — hell, it must be a seven-metre drop from the edge into the water — Neil then turned his attention to the other person. She stood only a metre or so from the edge, setting a bad example, her face also fixed on the ocean. Uninterested, perhaps even oblivious, to the exchange between father and son.

She wore a scarf to contain her blonde hair and big sunglasses — quite unnecessary, given the dense cloud cover — but from what he could see of her face, she looked young.

Early to mid-twenties, Neil guessed. Then again, in this golden age of genetics, who could be sure?

She was dressed in drab, heavy materials that concealed her body — skirt hem to her ankles, sleeves buttoned at the wrists. It went against the latest fashion. Her clothes were upmarket, as far as Neil could tell. That scarf, was it mink? Sable? Lab-born or the real thing? Whatever, Kim wouldn't be feeling anything like that around her neck any time soon, that was for sure.

She carried a rug, or a blanket. Lime green. A great heavy thing, clutched awkwardly up high on her shoulder. It seemed to weigh her down.

He approached his son, but kept his eyes on the woman. Did she look sad, he wondered, or did the downward curves of her small mouth reflect a more thoughtful expression? Hard to tell, and what did it matter to him anyway? He was just here for his boy, and to get him inside before the storm hit, as fast as his protesting thighs would allow.

He was only a couple of metres away when she turned her head to look in his direction. He smiled and she responded with the barest of nods.

'G'day,' Neil offered.

'Hello.'

She spoke softly, almost whispered the word. She raised her hand to tuck a loose strand of hair back beneath the scarf. At first, Neil thought she was offering it in greeting, so raised his own, but when he realised her real intention, he redirected, flicking his fingers in a gesture toward Paul.

'I hope he's not bothering you?'

She looked down at the boy, as if noticing him for the first time.

'No. Not at all,' she said.

'Ah... well, okay. Well, that's good.'

But she had already turned back to stare at the ocean. Fixated. That was the word. Worse than Paul. He couldn't see her eyes, but he was sure of their intensity, and the thought made him shiver a little. What was it about the view from up here? He turned to look out over the violent water. You couldn't see anything. It all came down to imagination, something Neil had never been good at. But Paul was a bright boy. That had been in the contract. Sometimes, he thought his son might be too smart for his own good, even when the specialists had promised him it was a necessity. This was a whole new world, centuries beyond the one he remembered.

Things changing. All the time.

Like the ocean, he supposed.

Neil returned to the woman. She hadn't moved. He felt the need to say something more, some polite banality, but her posture found him lacking the words. Best just to get his son and go.

'Paul,' he said.

He held out his hand. Paul took it, if reluctantly. Then Neil started to walk back the way he came, dragging that slight weight behind him.

'He's beautiful,' the woman said.

'Huh,' Neil said. More a grunt than a word. He turned back.

'Your son,' she said. 'He is your son? He's beautiful. He's perfect.'

Neil clenched his jaw. That word. The last one. What the hell did she mean by it? And how did she say it — sarcastic or... angry?

Neil tried, failed, then managed a stutter.

'Um... well, ahhh...?'

He had nothing.

The woman now turned her whole body, not just her head, to face him.

Confront him, it felt like.

Something in the bundled blanket on her shoulder moved. One of her hands gently patted it.

'I'm sorry,' she said. 'That must have sounded so rude. I apologise.'

'No, n-not at all...'

135

'All I mean is, and forgive me for asking, if he is your son, your biological son… he must have been… altered?'

Neil felt a cold, hard brick in his gut.

'Um… well, ah, yes, as it happens…'

He felt a heat in his face, much hotter than the sunburn. That was the new touchy subject; the one polite society never spoke about, and certainly not a topic to be discussed with a stranger.

Doesn't this rich bitch know the damn rules?

'Forgive me again,' she said, as if reading his mind. Now the bundle wriggled violently, more agitated this time. She hugged it a little closer, made *shhh* sounds, began to rock, ever so gently.

She looked back at Neil. She gave a tiny, almost embarrassed smile.

'Mine's altered too. He's a feisty one. So… independent, even at such a young age. But they all are, aren't they? I'm sure you understand.'

Neil reached desperately for something to say, found himself at a total loss. He was unsure if he should feel angry or apologetic. He felt resentment, certainly, but she seemed politely curious, after all. There seemed no mockery or animosity in her words, her posture.

Then again, what did he really know? He was never good at this. This was what his wife was for, but Kim was a long walk away. And she'd be worried. Neil desperately wanted to go, to run in fact, but he found himself rooted to the spot.

The wind off the sea grew stronger. The clouds reached lower. Thunder was insistent.

More blonde strands escaped from beneath the woman's scarf. This time, she didn't bother to tuck them back away, let them flail about her pretty face.

'Please,' she ventured, reading his awkward posture, 'I understand I'm being so terribly forward. But there is really no need to be embarrassed. We understand, don't we, you and I?'

Neil just gaped at her.

'We understand,' she continued, haltingly, choosing her words, 'the need to adapt... the... the urgency of the future. We only seek the best for our children, yes?'

Neil reached for his son, found his shoulder, gave it a squeeze. For a moment, he wondered if this was the right conversation to be having in front of him. Then he realised how ridiculous that thought was. His son was already smarter than he would ever be, and could explain the mechanics of his origins in such a scholarly manner, a way that made Neil uncomfortable whenever he heard it.

The procedure had begun while his son was still in the womb. It had cost a packet. They'd made the final repayments only late last year. And those endless conversations with Kim, the many arguments. She had been adamant. Slowly, with a will of iron, she had worn him down.

She'd been right of course. Neil was now sure of that... well, most of the time. A son with a stake in the future, uncomplicated by redundant genes. That's the word the consultant had used.

Many times.

Redundant.

And Neil. Who was he to contradict?

The boffins. They have our best interests at heart.

And now a son. A bright boy, if a little too bright, but one not prone to melancholy, only a stoic indifference that often was mistaken for it. A strong boy, no propensity to fat. A constitution shored up against the trammels of the mundane infections.

The other children. Emily and Tash?

Paul would be their shelter.

The gene for brotherly love. Neil had been adamant they wouldn't junk that one.

Now the thunder was booming. A fat drop of warm rain spattered Neil's cheek.

The bundle in the woman's arms was now thrashing, clearly agitated. She struggled with it, yet her voice stayed calm, as if there was no problem at all.

'Who knows the future?' she asked.

Rhetorical, Neil guessed. He said nothing.

'Can we really know, or must we only make our best predictions?'

Shit! Questions like this always found Neil out of his depth. He looked down again at his son. Paul had turned his attention to the contemplation of the churning sky.

She said: 'The world we know is…'

And now the bundle in the woman's arms gave a jolt. The blanket began to shred. A flailing arm broke free, made a thin red line in her neck. The rain slanted in, obscuring Neil's vision.

Just a glimpse. Scales. Webbed digits. A grey-green complexion.

The woman fell back. Her throat was now red mayhem. Too late, Neil scrambled for her rescue. She was on the ground, the bundle undulating beside her, jerking with hidden menace.

The child emerged.

Neil bit back a surge of bile.

Slim, compact. Thin skin, lidless eyes for deep exploration. A batrachian design. Thick blood. A heart that waits.

Waits for the downfall of redundant species.

The newborn scrambled toward the edge of the retaining wall. It was ungainly, out of its element. Neil watched it flounder. The woman still twitched, but he had already forgotten her. Paul, on the edge of his gaping vision, had fallen to his hands and knees, much like a supplicant. He moved toward it, a penitent, in the wake of the new Messiah. Neil was too weak, the rain too hammering, to offer any admonishment. He was beaten. The world was no longer his world.

The phone in his pocket, ringing. Kim. Worried. He ignored it.

And Paul. The best son money could buy. The confident hope, now just a muddy, sodden acolyte. All that hard work, the soul searching, and already surpassed.

The newborn reached the brink. It paused, turned back briefly. Raised an arm. A benediction? Paul just might hope so in the years to come.

Then it slipped over the edge and was gone.

Paul might have wept, but he was made better than that. He looked to his father, that irrational prototype. That bag of junk genes. Another time, and maybe, maybe, there might have been the possibility for familial considerations.

But Paul lived on the cusp of the future. There was no time.

'Why?' he asked.

And his sire, a blubbering mess. Tears awash in the rain.

'Why couldn't you have made me beautiful?'

THE HUNT
Mark Smith-Briggs

The prints were fresh. They tracked from the muddy edge of the dam into the nearby scrub. If Todd had to guess, he'd say they were less than an hour old.

'Holy shit,' he said and ran his finger around the edge of the indent. The rear pad was shaped roughly like a bell and topped by four, pebble-like toes.

Josh rested the butt of his rifle against his hip and took a swig from his flask. 'What'd you think?' he asked.

Todd ran through his usual checklist. They were too big for a domestic cat — even the feral ones — and there were no claw marks, which ruled out dogs. Judging by the diameter and depth of the indent, whatever made them was about seventy kilos and the size of a large bulldog.

Todd smiled. After a decade of searching, they were so close he could almost taste it.

'I think we're about to make fucking history,' he said.

In reply, the sky rumbled with distant thunder. Dark clouds were beginning to roll across the horizon. Josh eyed them with concern.

'Let's get going before that storm sets in,' he said. 'If those prints get washed away, we've got squat.'

They followed the tracks deeper into the bush. Recent rains had left the ground soft, so it was easy to follow the animal's ascent into the mountain range. Still, it took the best part of the afternoon. The trail led them halfway up the mountain before disappearing into the mouth of a cave. Todd rested against a tree trunk to catch his breath. Overhead, the sky had turned a bleak grey.

Josh dumped his pack on the ground but kept his rifle trained on the opening in the rock face.

'So what now?' he asked.

'We go in, I guess,' Todd said.

'Are you mad? It's pitch fucking black in there.'

Todd shrugged.

'We could always chuck a flare in, try to flush it out.'

'Or scare it in further.'

'Well, I ain't standing out here all day.'

Josh paused, mulling things over. Finally, he bent down and fished a flare out of his pack. He held it out for his friend.

Todd shook his head and tapped his rifle. 'You do it. I've got your back.'

Josh muttered something under his breath, but grabbed a lighter from his pocket and crept toward the cave anyway. He paused at the opening; close enough so that its shadow touched his shoe.

'Do it,' Todd urged.

He raised the unlit flare to the edge of the darkness and sparked the Zippo. A pair of yellow eyes reflected back from the darkness. Josh barely registered the rush of a shadow — black on black — before something slammed into him.

The shape hit him hard enough to knock the wind from his

lungs and drove him backwards into the dirt. He groaned as the full weight of it bore down. Razor sharp claws punctured his skin. It growled and gnashed at him with long, jagged teeth.

Todd watched in a state of shock. The black cat — it was waist height at least — tore at the flesh of Josh's chest and arms. On instinct more than anything, Todd fired.

The bullet tore into the cat's flesh just below its shoulder. The animal shrieked in pained surprise but continued its attack. He cracked off another shot. It too hit the mark. The animal made a high-pitch sound and bounded into the bush.

Todd watched it disappear into the scrub. 'Did you see that?' he said to no one in particular. 'I fucking knew it.'

Josh gave a pained groan.

'Oh, shit,' Todd said and rushed to his side. His friend's shirt was slick with blood. The worst damage appeared to have been done to his left forearm, which had deep puncture wounds from where he had tried to keep the cat away from his throat. He rolled onto his stomach and hacked up a string of bloody mucus.

'Oh, man, we've got to get you help,' Todd said. He pulled out his phone. No bars. 'Shit!'

He grabbed Josh by the arm and dragged him to his feet. Josh collapsed onto his shoulder but managed to stay upright.

'Was it?' he asked.

'Yeah,' Todd said.

'You going after it?'

Todd scanned the scrub. He'd hit the thing twice and it

wasn't likely to make it far. If they brought back a body…

Josh coughed up a fresh wad of blood and slunk further onto Todd's shoulder.

Todd sighed. They were knee-deep in the middle of nowhere, and if Josh didn't get help fast, his chances weren't so flash either. But it would take a few hours to hike back down at best. The first of several fat drops of rain splashed onto his foot.

'Forget it,' he said reluctantly.

#

They came across the house an hour later. Both were drenched and close to collapse. It was a small mud-brick dwelling nestled deep within the trees. A narrow track wound its way to the front door. It was so well hidden that they would have missed it entirely had it not been for a piece of rusted corrugated roof sheeting banging in the breeze.

Josh was beginning to dip in and out of consciousness. Todd knew there was no way he was going to make it back down to the bottom without medical aid.

'Come on,' Todd said, leading them up the path.

The door was answered by a slender, dark-haired woman. She was attractive, in her late forties or early fifties, with olive skin and magnetic, brown eyes. She eyed the pair cautiously.

'Please,' Todd said before she had a chance to shut the door again. 'You have to help me, my friend, he's been hurt.'

144

Todd noticed her gaze linger, not so much on the blood but his rifle.

'What happened?' she said at last.

'He was attacked.'

'Attacked?'

'By a black cat. A panther.'

Todd expected her to laugh, or slam the door in his face. Most people did when he brought up the topic. The Australian bush was full of tales of such sightings, but there was no real proof. He and Josh had dedicated most of the past decade to trying to find some. Today, he found it. But at what cost?

The woman didn't laugh or slam the door. Instead, Todd noticed a genuine flicker of fear in her eyes. She stole a glance back inside the house. When she looked back, her face had softened.

'Quick, inside,' she said hurriedly. 'But the gun stays out here.'

The woman took Josh's arm around her shoulder and helped him into the house. Todd couldn't help but notice the way her dress clung to her rounded hips.

'Here,' she said, helping Josh into a wooden chair. 'He's lost a lot of blood, yes?'

Todd nodded. 'I guess.'

She removed the clotted jacket from Josh's arm.

'You said a panther did this?'

Todd nodded again.

'This is very bad,' she said and disappeared into the next room.

145

Josh took the moment to take in his surroundings. The room was small but homely and served as both a living room and dining area. A kitchenette ran along the back wall. There was no TV or other modern appliances in sight.

The woman rushed back in from the hallway carrying a water bowl and cloth. She juggled a series of small vials under one arm. She laid them out on the table and handed Todd a pair of scissors. 'Here, cut away the fabric from around the wounds so I can clean them.'

Todd did as she said. Josh grimaced as he plucked the blood soaked fabric from his arm and chest. The woman used the cloth to gently wash away the blood.

When they were done, she wrapped the wounds in a white bandage. Together they helped Josh over to the couch.

She opened one of the vials and tipped a small amount of the purple coloured liquid into a glass. It smelled faintly of flowers. She lifted the glass to Josh's lips.

'Drink,' she said.

'What is it?' Todd asked.

'An old family recipe,' she said. 'To help him sleep.'

She left the room again and returned with a blanket, flannel shirt and pants.

'My husband's… or they were,' she said.

She handed Todd the clothes and covered Josh with the blanket. He closed his eyes and began to doze.

Todd checked for bars of reception on his mobile. Nothing.

'We need to get him to a hospital,' he said, shoving the

phone back into his pocket. 'Do you have a phone?'

'No,' she said.

'A car?'

Again the woman shook her head. 'My sons do,' she offered. 'But they won't be back 'til later. Your friend needs rest. Best you wait out the storm here.'

She went into the kitchen and produced a bottle of scotch and two glasses from a cupboard. She brought them over to the table and sat down on the chair opposite him. She poured two shots — neat, no ice — and handed one to Todd.

'To help with the shock,' she said.

#

Before he knew it, half the bottle was gone and a haze had settled about the room. Outside, the storm continued to rage, but inside, with the warmth of hard liquor in his belly, things didn't seem so bad. Even Josh, who had tossed about in small fits at first, now rested peacefully.

The woman, whom Todd had learned was named Veronica, was no stranger to stories about black cats.

'The bush holds many secrets,' she said. 'And yes, I believe they are one of them.'

'Have you ever seen one?' Todd asked.

The woman shook her head. But something in her eyes said she was holding something back.

The room fell into an awkward silence. Todd poured each another drink. They sipped it in silence.

On the couch, Josh groaned and shifted in his sleep.

'He needs a hospital,' Todd said.

'I know.'

'Your sons, will they be back soon?'

Veronica looked longingly out the window. 'Soon enough.'

Another long moment of silence passed. Finally, Veronica brought her gaze back from outside and smiled. 'But let's not dwell. It's rare that I get to enjoy company out here.'

Todd felt the brush of her foot on his inner leg. It moved upward toward his thigh. He flinched and excused himself for the bathroom. Veronica sighed and pointed down the hall.

'Last door on the right,' she said.

Todd relieved himself and spent a long time in front of the basin mirror. His eyes were bloodshot and the room swam in and out of focus. He splashed water on his face. *Okay. Pull your head in. You're drunk. Josh is hurt. Probably dying. And she's nearly old enough to be your mother.* He felt the beginnings of an erection stir in his pants. *Shit.*

He stumbled back out into the hall and used a hand to steady himself on the wall. A bedroom door on his right was slightly ajar.

Todd glimpsed a teenage boy lying in a bed. He was drenched in sweat and tossed fitfully beneath the sheets. Bandages covered most of his upper torso and there were two red spots where the blood had soaked through.

Todd felt a hand on his shoulder and jumped. It was

Veronica.

'What…' he began.

She stepped forward and thrust her lips against his. He felt her tongue, probing, as she reached behind and closed the door. He kissed her back and was pushed across the hall into her bedroom.

#

Afterward, they collapsed in an exhausted tangle among the sheets. He rested his head on one of her bare breasts and listened to the beat of her heart. She exhaled and gently stroked the back of his sweaty hair. The past half-hour had been a frantic, almost animalistic, grind of flesh against flesh. But now an eerie calm washed over the room. Todd closed his eyes and listened to the soothing sound of rain on the tin roof. His thoughts drifted back to the boy in the room. He turned to ask Veronica about his wounds but fell asleep before the thought could pass to his lips.

#

He woke groggily to a darkened room. His head pounded with the onset of a full-blown hangover. He groaned and rubbed his eyes with one hand. It took a moment to remember where he was. He smiled and reached across the bed but found nothing but cotton.

Maybe she was tending to the boy.

Todd frowned. Slowly, he swung his feet over the edge of the bed and found the floorboards with his feet. Something cold and sharp jerked taut against his wrist. What the fuck? He reached down and felt the circular link of metal; tried to pull his hand away and heard the jangle of steel links. Handcuffs.

They hadn't been there before he went to sleep. Had they?

He used his free hand to search around the bed. Maybe the key was somewhere among the sheets. His fingers brushed a smooth plastic object. He recognised it immediately. But what the hell was it doing in the bed? He picked it up, instinctively sliding his thumb across the small glass screen. His phone's home screen filled the room with soft light. It was bare except for the bed and a chest of drawers on the far wall. The bedroom door was shut.

He turned his attention back to the phone. How the hell did it get here? It had been in his pants. Wet clothes which he had changed out of when...

He checked the top corner of the screen. A single bar of reception was showing. He pressed the phone icon and selected the recent calls list. There was a bunch of calls, four or five of them to an unfamiliar number. The first appeared to have been made shortly after they had arrived, probably just after he had got changed, the last less than an hour ago. But who had she been calling?

His finger hovered over the redial button. Don't be stupid.

Instead, he punched in 000.

A footstep creaked on the floorboards at the end of the hall. Todd felt his breath catch in the back of his throat and put the phone face down on the bed to cut out the light. Slowly, deliberately, the footsteps approached along the hall.

They paused outside the bedroom. Todd heard the squeak of the door handle, followed by the creak of the door itself. A crack of dim light crept across the room.

He pushed the phone under his naked thigh; the emergency number idle on the screen. The door opened further, bathing the bed in light.

Veronica stood in the doorway. She was naked and splattered in what looked like blood.

'Good. You're awake,' she said.

A pair of large black cats appeared by her side. They purred and rubbed affectionately against her knees.

Todd felt his breath catch in his throat. They were near identical to the one he had shot earlier. The same blood-like splatter coated their teeth and jaws.

Todd thought of his friend asleep in the lounge.

'Where's Josh?' he asked. In his gut, he already knew the answer.

Veronica simply smiled.

'You bitch!' he screamed and struggled against the restraints.

The cats let out an agitated growl and began to pace. Veronica soothed them with a pat on the head.

'Now, now,' she said. 'It's for the best really. He'd been bit and it was only a matter of time.'

Todd fought back tears. Whether they were for him or his friend he didn't know.

'For what?' he said.

'You really don't know?' she said, a tinge of disappointment in her voice. 'I thought you'd figured it out.'

She dropped her hands to her side, letting them rest on each of the panthers' heads.

Todd watched the way they nuzzled against her touch.

'Your sons,' he said.

She nodded gently, letting it sink in.

Todd's mind raced with possibilities. He thought of the boy in the other bedroom. Of the bullet-shaped blood stains. If they were her sons, her real biological sons, that would mean... The room swam suddenly and a wave of bile rose in the back of his throat. He choked it down.

Veronica watched him patiently, like a kinder teacher waiting on a small child.

He toyed with the word for ages. Tried it out on his tongue. It was impossible, wasn't it?

'Werewolves,' he said at last.

Veronica shrugged. 'Werecats, if you want to be so rudimentary. That's a term created by your kind to label what you don't understand.' She took a step into the room. Her sons followed.

Todd pulled at his wrist; tried to squeeze it through the metal cuff. His hand slipped part way through and caught on his thumb.

'The Aborigines often thought of us as a type of bunyip,' she said. 'White men made up stories about escaped panthers from travelling zoos. The truth is we have been here, living

152

among you, all this time.'

She smiled, a sad, pitiful look, and glanced back toward the door across the hall.

'You didn't think I could let you get away with it, did you?'

Todd tugged at the cuff and felt his thumb starting to push through.

'But why wait?' he said, stalling, desperate to get his hand free. 'Why not kill us before?'

'We like to do things as a family. Besides, you had other uses.'

She patted at her belly lovingly. 'The boys' father was a hunter just like you. He never got to meet them though.'

Todd remembered the pants and shirt she had given him and shuddered.

'Then again, neither will you,' she snapped.

Veronica's eyes flashed a bright yellow and she dropped forward onto all fours.

Todd watched her skin darken as her body morphed into a sleek, predatory beast. She snarled, that seductive smile replaced by a mouth full of jagged teeth.

She pounced.

Todd barely registered the crack as his thumb snapped and his hand finally slipped free. He was able to raise it just far enough to feel the silky brush of her fur as she landed on top of him.

THE MONSTER IN THE WOODS
Kathryn Hore

When they came to take her, she screamed and screamed and screamed.

Though she witnessed the ballot herself, all their attempts to be fair. In that long room stinking of rank fear and sweat, the village adults hovering close and clutching hands while up front the town elders stood, looking as stricken as any. The mayor, the doctor, the notary. Lord Greswold himself, owner of almost all the land hereabouts. The men who were meant to protect them.

Standing on the outer, she watched as they dragged forward the big box containing the name of every eligible adult. She saw with her own eyes the lord reaching within to choose. You couldn't get more random than that, even she had to agree. You couldn't get fairer.

Still, when they came for her, she screamed.

'Don't do this, you bastards. Greswold! You can't do this!'

They did not listen. Refused to look her in the eye. The biggest men of the village, farmers, builders, all thick arms and grim lips, coming for her. It took four of them to restrain her, pulling her forward, grabbing her waist, her legs, one man to each arm. She tried to fight, to hit and punch and kick. When they wrapped their strength about her limbs, she tried to bite instead. When they managed to keep beyond reach of her teeth, she simply screamed.

Loud enough for all to hear.

Loud enough to wake the children.

The other adults kept back, watching without word. Condoning, approving. Not one stepping forward as she was dragged into the night, not a single voice raised in protest, surely this is wrong? Was that surprising? Was she really so friendless? These people came to her for advice when they were ill, when they were worried, when they were infertile and the town doctor was of little use. They thought her the keeper of some arcane knowledge and she let them, because an esoteric image could be useful. She never told them she simply read the same books their doctor studied from, mixed in some local knowledge of the herbs hereabouts and was prepared to think more broadly than the stiff old physician ever bothered to.

They came to her when their children were ill. When they were desperate. She helped them.

Didn't they understand she wanted to save them too, the children? She wanted to find a way. But this wasn't it, this couldn't be it. Blood for blood, it could not work.

But the townspeople looked on without pity, silent as the men dragged her away. She begged for help, but their eyes reflected only relief that it was not them.

She screamed.

A backhand to the jaw knocked the sound out of her. Teeth clattering, head knocking back. Black clouds edged her vision; it was all she could do keep conscious. Her limbs went slack and she struggled to remember where and when she was, what was happening, who or why.

They carried her forward, passing buildings, houses. A rough road beneath their feet. The night becoming thick as they left the town behind. Ahead, tiny pinprick lights danced in the dark. Torches carried by the four old men, Lord Greswold leading the way. And beyond them, a looming darkness.

Greswold led them to it. Down into the woods.

'This won't save them. Please,' she tried as the trees grew closer and the path twisted in. Her throat was hoarse and it came out as a whisper; something they could ignore as the forest closed around them. It was thick amid the trees. A blanket darkness barely held at bay by their torches, branches reaching out in clutching tangles. The old men lit the way down the narrow, twisting path, the younger following with her tight in their arms. They would not leave the path, not even these men, the town's strongest. None would dare step amid the trees at night.

She began to struggle again as the path spilled into an open space; a clearing lost in the woods. Claustrophobic with trees towering in a ring, the barest hint of black sky glimpsed through matted branches above. She jerked a leg. She yanked an arm, and managed to get it free. She started hitting out, but they ignored each feeble blow. Senses returning, she felt the scream build again in her throat.

'Keep her quiet,' the doctor hissed. He sounded nervous, even to her ears.

"'Tis easy for you,' a young man snapped back, but got his hand over her mouth. He clamped her lips tight with his calloused fingers so she couldn't even bite him.

In the middle of the clearing was a pole. Tall and wooden,

driven deep into the ground; they had prepared for this, set it all up, and now they dragged her to it. There was rope already attached to the pole and she felt it looped first about an ankle. They pulled it tight, until it cut deep into her flesh.

She cried out, cursing them with the pain.

Another loop went about her waist, then one around each wrist. She thrashed about, but they roped her so no limb was free. She was trapped. Tied in the woods in the middle of the night, a sacrifice given up to the dark.

She knew what happened to sacrifices in these woods. Blood on the ground and torn flesh. So did the men. When they staggered back from her, four old, four young, their expressions were aghast. Faces lit by torchlight as they stared at their handiwork, made all the more dreadful for the shadows.

'You think this will save them? Your children?' she cried out.

One young man, a farmer, stepped forward.

'Something must be done,' he said. He sounded afraid, but she had little pity for his fear. 'We can't let it take our kids.'

'It will anyway. Sacrifice won't stop it. We need another way.'

'It wants blood. We have to give it someone...'

'We don't know what it wants!' she tried. 'That's what we need to find out.'

Lord Greswold put a hand on the man's arm and pulled him back. 'Don't listen to her. She knows nothing.'

'Greswold, you bastard. You know no more!'

But she did not waste time on him, it had been too many years since she'd wasted time on him and the history between

157

them was too old for it to even hurt anymore.

Instead, she turned back to the farmers. To those she thought might listen.

'If we can figure out why it's come, we can figure out a way to stop it,' she said. But their expressions remained stolid.

She tried reason, then anger, then fear, pleading with them at the last. But they turned their backs. Two picked up torches; Greswold and the doctor. The mayor and the notary left theirs, allowing her some light, even if only enough to create more shadows. She watched their backs, desperate to get away, hurrying down the path.

'You bastards!' she screamed. 'This isn't the end of it. Your children won't be safe. The monster in these woods will take them still!'

But they were gone, leaving her roped and alone, with only fear and shadows for company.

She allowed herself some tears. A damp bitterness on her cheeks, a salt taste on her tongue. For a moment she was stuck, by the ropes, by her own impotent fury. By the growing terror which wrapped itself around her gut and squeezed. They did not have a name for what was in these woods; to name such a thing brought its own danger. But they had chronicled its impact. The occasional survivor, rare and mute, trembling wrecks of people who never recovered any sense. The rest, the others, every traveller through these woods after dark. Left as little more than piles of torn flesh atop blood-soaked earth.

Except for the children. The children were never found. Never seen again.

And then the children had begun disappearing from within

the town. From within their very own beds.

She did not blame the townspeople their fear. She had no children and perhaps they thought she did not understand, but she did. Really she did. Only it was her name pulled from the box, her body tied out here in the night with the shadows reaching. She was the one they were giving up to the woods, their sacrifice, given to suffer for their children.

Damn it. She had to stop crying. She had to do something.

She sniffed back the tears and tried to inspect her bonds. The knots were tight, but they were only knots. Tied by men who were strong, but afraid and desperate to get away, rushing too quickly to check their handiwork. Surely she could find a loose slip in one of the knots, a catch in the ropes she could work to her advantage.

She picked with one hand at the ropes around the other. As she did, she heard the trees behind her sway.

Her head snapped up. Every nerve in her body froze. Even the breath in her throat was still as she focused her listening.

Nothing.

Then something.

A shift in the trees. Movement. In the distance.

Coming closer.

She turned back to the knotted rope with renewed scrambling. Frantic, pulling with her nails, her fingers, her teeth. Blinking rapidly to clear her vision; the tears were back, but this time they were of panic and she paid them no heed. The ropes around her right wrist held. She gave it up and switched hands, trying to work at her left instead.

A finger caught under the edge of the rope. Her breath

caught with it.

She heard rustling behind her. Her chest tightened, dropped into her gut.

Yanking, pulling. Her skin tearing with it, under the ropes. She barely noticed, kicking at the pole instead, grunting with effort as she wrenched hard and felt something give way.

Her left hand tore free. It allowed slack in the rope and with frenzied movement she pulled again at the knots at her right. Breaking nails, burning skin, she managed to get it loose. Ropes were everywhere, around her waist, her ankles, but she tried to shake them off, tried to get a foot out.

Something. Something moving in the trees.

Something stepping into the clearing behind her.

The torch-lit shadows stretching before her shifted. Something moving in front of the light. The skin beneath her hair crawled and she heard a terrified sound, realising only distantly it was from her own throat. And bonds only partially loosened or not, she tried her best to run.

She bolted toward the path, shaking off the remaining rope as she did so.

Her left ankle slid out beneath her. Still tied too tight.

She cried out as she fell and hit the ground hard. Her shoulder, her hip. The thump of it took the breath out of her and left her wheezing in the dirt. She heaved back into winded lungs, gasping for air as she lay on the ground. Too long. She had to get up. Struggling for breath, twisting to reach for her ankle. But the ropes cut in too tight and the knots held. Brutal spikes of pain shot through her leg as she yanked at it. The joint was twisted.

No. No, she couldn't let it take her. She couldn't die here and let the townsfolk get away with doing this to her.

A shadow fell across the ground. A darkness over her body. It brought cold. She shivered. She had to draw her hands together to stop their shake.

'Please,' she whispered, not daring to look up. 'Please. Just... please.'

'Yes. They do often plead.'

The voice was smooth. Deep and resonant, it sounded a vibration low in her gut. Despite herself, she began to look up. She had to see. She wanted to know. What manner of thing could speak so? Her eyes lifted slowly and she told herself not to scream, no matter what she saw there. Whatever the horrific visage or inhuman dread made solid, whatever abomination that was the monster in these woods.

It was a man.

A handsome one, at that. Leaning one shoulder against the pole, muscled arms bare and crossed over a vest, looking down at her. The kind of man that had always caught her eye. Shadows played havoc with the features of his face. He seemed to have blonde hair, or maybe it was brown. His arms were strong, thick, his torso solid; there was a strength in him, a raw masculinity to his broad shoulders. In the semi-darkness, it seemed his eyes were only black.

She closed her eyes and wiped them with torn fingers. When she opened them again, he was still there. Still the same, unmoved and unimpressed by her pleas.

'Who are you?' she asked, a breathless sound, because she wasn't sure what else to say.

He grinned. She had the fleeting impression the teeth in his mouth were sharp.

'They see what they want. What they fear most. Or want most. Or both,' he said. His voice rattled in her head. It seemed to contain its own echo. 'Not often do they see a man.'

She felt herself swallow. Her throat was suddenly dry.

'It is a mask,' she said. 'This before me, what I see. So it is a mask.'

The man shrugged, uninterested in her attempts to make sense of what was happening. It seemed to bore him. He stood straight and came toward her. She shied back, a cowering movement she immediately regretted, but he did not attempt to touch her. He only stood above and looked down.

'And never,' he said, 'do they ask the right questions.'

She had to stop staring. Lying sprawled on the ground in his shadow, gazing up with breathless wonder. He was tall above her, and when he moved, she saw the muscles in his arms flex, the strength of his shoulders, torchlight and shadow against skin. It brought a gasp to her throat, an unwitting catch to her breath as she stared and could not stop. Could not tear her eyes away.

Move — she must move. Anything to shake some sense back into herself. She made herself stand, despite the pain shooting up from her ankle and the stinging burns from the rope. It was a slow process with little grace, wobbling lopsided to her feet bit by bit. But it got her up. It let her hobble backwards as far as the rope would allow her. It stopped her crouching in his shadow.

More importantly, it made her eyes turn away. Even still,

she could not stop thinking of those arms. What would they be like held about her? What would the touch of his hands, firm with intent, feel like against her skin?

No. He was no man.

'What are you?'

His laughter echoed low. 'You would not want to know. Be satisfied with what you see.'

She fought to hold her ground as he stepped closer. She shook, but would not turn, not even as the space between them diminished. He came so close she could feel his breath cool on her cheek, the shifting strength of his body in the wake of her own. She had to fight an inexplicable urge to reach out and touch him.

He bent his head to her ear. She did not pull away.

'What do you want?' he whispered.

'Me?' she breathed, trying to clear her head. It was fuzzy. Hard to think with him so close. 'No. Wait. What do you want? I should be asking...'

He shifted again, his body almost touching hers. Stepping behind her, moving around her, shifting near. She stayed very still. Waiting. She wasn't sure why, for him to grab her maybe. To touch her. Perhaps to tear her apart. To do whatever he desired. Her breath was short, fast, coming in gasps. Her every muscle was yearning toward him. No, not waiting; anticipating.

He did not touch her. He did not bridge the final inch between them.

She felt his lips by her other ear. 'Then ask.'

'What... what is it you want?'

She heard that laughter again. A rumble through her limbs.

'It is not I who wants.'

She tried to lift her chin, find defiance. Found herself leaning back toward him instead. She should be struggling, fighting, not just standing waiting for him to touch her. She saw him raise a hand. He brought it close to her face, her cheek. She braced herself, thought finally. Leaned her head back as if already under his hold.

His skin did not brush hers. His fingers hovered millimetres from her face, but kept at that same distance as he traced them down the line of her chin, her throat, her shoulder. Her body, her breasts, her waist. Her hip. Maddening. She wanted to cry out at him, she wanted to scream: touch me!

She forced a breath back and turned to look straight into those midnight black eyes.

'Is that...' she began, then had to stop, swallow, start again. 'Is that all you are? A temptation made flesh? A trick of the mind seducing me?'

His lips twisted in the shadows; a smile, sharp like his teeth.

'If such is a trick, it is a good one, no?'

His voice vibrated her core. She found herself leaning toward it. It was all she could do not to clutch him.

'I should be fighting you. I should be running from you.'

'Then fight. Run. But why worry about should? Focus instead on want.'

'What do I want?'

She wasn't sure why she asked that. The words were out of her mouth before she could consider them.

'Now you are asking the right questions.'

He turned, a languid movement, stepping away. An emptiness left behind, the feeling of something lost.

As he moved, he raised a hand, held it up. Around his wrist something weaved. Silk. Silk cuffs, ravelling, pulling together, cloth stitching around him even as she watched, spun from the air, from the darkness and shadows. Down his arms, a fine jacket in green appeared stitch by stitch across those broad shoulders. It was fitted and trimmed. The other arm held out, he turned, cocked his head as the cloth stitched its way about him, down his body, covering his skin. Jacket and shirt, belt and pants. Thick, leather boots, polished and expensive, with silver buckles gleaming bright.

A hat. Bowing his head, a cane forming in one hand. When he raised his head again, when he tipped that hat to her, it was with a very familiar face.

'Greswold' she said and heard the disgust in her own voice.

But this was not the Greswold of now. This was the Greswold of the past. Brown hair not yet greyed, round face not yet lined. Muscular shoulders and youthful strength; yes, he'd had those once. There had been attractions. It had been many years since she'd seen that one so young, and maybe back then it had been different, but now all it did was bring a sour taste to her mouth.

Her jaw clenched, she felt herself shift back. It was Greswold who looked at her, but that smile was still sharp and those eyes were still black.

'Greswold is not what I want,' she said.

'You did once.'

'A long time ago. I learned my lesson.'

The sharp grin grew. 'But not the right one.'

A raised hand lashed out. She was beyond arm's reach, too far away for it to connect. But it did not need to. It was enough that it once had.

It wasn't that she felt the slap; she remembered it. The stinging open palm blow to her cheek, the shock and shame flooding through her with it. Her head flicked back, a grunt passing her lips. She was pushed back a step by the force of it.

She gasped. A memory should never hurt so much.

He stood several feet from her. But she felt the grip around her wrist now just as she had then and she fought against it now as then too. Crying out, yanking herself back. This wasn't happening, this wasn't now. She fought to tell herself that. This was then, back when they were young, little more than teenagers. Back when he'd been just another village kid, if one with fierce ambition, and she a young fool attracted by good looks and charm alone.

The grip about her waist bit in, held by hands she could not see but only remember. She twisted in them, fighting, yanking herself away. Forming a fist, lashing out with her arms. She felt her punch connect. She heard the ghost whispers of his cursing on the wind.

She turned to run. Back then she had run.

The rope tugged back on her ankle and she cried out with the agony of it, staggering forward. The spikes of pain bolted up her leg and shocked the memory, if such was what it was, as physical as it was, away.

She found herself panting, gulping back breath. Untouched

and standing in the night, shaking with the adrenalin of a struggle which had happened twenty years before. She had got away then. She had assumed it was over, done with. Had she been wrong in that?

She looked back over her shoulder, her face still stinging from the slap of long ago. It was no longer Greswold there. He had returned to his first appearance, that strength of man, and she could not have said she was sorry. Perhaps this creature with his hungry black eyes pulled her forward too easily, but she would take that over Greswold any day.

And yet there was something of Greswold which remained. Before the creature was a box. A great wooden box, just like the one she had watched the lord take a name from. The one from which he had pulled her own name.

She eyed it with suspicion. It could not be real. 'What...' she began, but her words dragged off. Instead, she stepped forward, limping, trying to ignore the low burning of suspicion deep inside her.

'There is a price for knowing,' he told her. 'Are you sure this is what you want?'

She said nothing, just kept shuffling to that box. She could see the little bits of twisted card inside, innocuous as they lay there. Folded over so she could not read them. She stared at them. Raised a hand. Hesitated.

Her eyes flicked upward. He was watching her. Black eyes waiting. Hungry.

She plunged her hand amid the cards. It felt real and her fingers closed around something. She pulled a tiny piece of card out and flicked it open.

Her name was written across it.

But of course. That made sense. It had been her name.

She let the card drop, let it flutter to the ground, and looked up to stare at him. He said nothing, only waited while she made her decisions.

Quicker now, staring at him still, she plunged her hand back among the cards. Pulled out another and tore it open.

Her name again.

And again.

And again.

'No.'

Again.

'No!'

She yanked at the box with both hands as the bile rose up in her throat. The box was solid, heavy, all too real. It rocked as she grabbed it, pushed it. It fell with a thud, spilling its contents across the dirt. All those innocuous bits of card, all those secrets, scattered across the forest floor.

'No!' she cried out, as one after the other, those bits of cards showed her own name.

She yanked herself away, staggering, stumbling. Barely staying upright, standing in the middle of the clearing, shaking and clenching her fists, the truth too hard, too bitter.

'It was meant to be fair,' she said, as if that made a difference. 'It was meant to be...'

But what did that even mean, fair? The selection of a sacrifice in some equitable manner all would accept? As if that could make it right. As if that changed anything. She was still the body given to suffer, still the one they gave up to the beast.

He was still standing, waiting, patient.

'Why?' she cried. 'Why are you here? Why do you show me this?'

'I come when called.' He shifted, moved behind her, beyond her vision. She saw him reappear from the corner of her other eye. 'I take what is given.'

'The children are not given! They are not…'

But her words dragged off. She thought of the bits of card. Her eyes clenched shut, tight enough to squeeze back the tears. She wanted to shake the suspicion from her head and refuse the possibility. There were too many secrets here which should never be found out. She told herself she no longer wanted to know them. That she no longer wanted to know any of it.

That was a lie. The truth was still the biggest temptation of all.

He stepped around in front of her. He held out one hand, one long muscled arm.

'Come,' he said. 'Come and find out what you really want.'

Her own hands were sweaty and she wiped them against her skirts. 'I do not want to die,' she said, because that much was truth she could be sure of. 'I do not want to be torn apart.'

'You will not mind. It is but a price.'

There seemed no options, no escapes. Yet he did nothing but hold out a hand. Waiting with the patience of one who knows the conclusion is forgone. She could not deny the heat which rose to her cheeks, the warmth low down in her belly as she looked back at him. She could not deny just how much she really wanted, even if she wasn't quite sure what.

Come and find out. The gesture seemed to offer answers, explanations. Perhaps it also offered pain and death. The unknown made her insides turn, though she did not back away. She understood this was her choice. She had not expected that. Her choice. And so she chose.

She raised a shaking hand and put her clammy fingers into his.

A sound rose up out of her, a cry in the night. She tried to pull her hand away again, but once in his hold, he did not give it up. His grip was cold, icily burning. The piercing of a thousand needles into her skin. It felt as if the flesh of her fingers was searing, tearing. As if it were ripping away from her bones.

She cried out and gripped tighter. And the instant her skin touched his, she knew.

Around her in the clearing, she saw it. The past, the truth. The young Greswold cursing her own retreating form, running from him and leaving him furious, thwarted. She had not given him what he wanted. His blame lashed out at her, at everyone. At the town itself. Hunched over in these woods, calling out his wants to the night.

She heard his cries on the wind. Power. Wealth. Land. Always the same. Power. Of course.

She heard another come to bring answer to his desires. What would you give to have what you want?

Greswold hadn't even hesitated.

The first born of all who owe me allegiance.

And in the darkness of the wood, she cried with the sadness of it and the pain, grabbed at her own wrist, and pulled.

The contact broke. She went stumbling back, numbed hand clutched to her, staggering on her injured ankle. She fell to her knees, heaving nausea, the truth sitting rancid in her belly. It rose up her throat and she leaned over, coughing, retching. Spitting out strands of foul-tasting bile, bitter tears mixing with vomit. Heaving over and over again.

She threw it all up, but she could not conquer this knowing.

Silence. She shivered in it for a long time. Thinking of Greswold. Of the town which would make her their sacrifice. Thinking of the children. After a while, she raised her good hand to wipe at her eyes, her mouth; the other remained useless and damaged in her lap. The price of knowing, of wanting to know. It begged a question, what would be the price for something even more?

When she glanced back over her shoulder, he was still there. Black eyes watching. Waiting. Interesting, but she no longer felt afraid.

'I know what I want,' she said. Her voice sounded raw.

'Yes.'

'And you will give it to me?'

'Yes.'

'For a price?'

'There is always a price.'

She nodded and pushed herself to her feet, balancing on her good ankle. For a moment, she looked at him in the semi-darkness, the torchlight and shadows competing across his skin. Taking in the strength of his jaw, the breadth of his shoulders, the power in his arms and hands. She thought again

171

of what it would feel like to have those hands on her body, her skin. His lips at her neck, her shoulders. Her breasts. Her thighs. Impossible to deny she wanted it. She thought of his teeth sharp against her flesh, but she did not think she would mind.

She moved to stand in front of him. He did not try to touch her. He had only ever offered.

'I want...' she began, but stopped. It was important to get this right. She wanted many things, including this visage of him, but she had long ago learned that good-looking, powerful men were rarely worth the price they demanded.

And what she was prepared to pay for was something else entirely.

In her head, she heard echoes of her own cries. If we know why it's come, we can know how to stop it... She knew why now. She even knew how to stop it.

But it was too late for that.

'I want,' she said and he nodded. He knew exactly what she wanted.

She lifted both hands to his face, leaned forward and kissed him.

His lips were cold. She dropped her hands to his shoulders and pushed aside his vest. His body beneath was searing with the freeze. It numbed her fingers, froze her hands. His tongue was ice in her mouth. She felt cold hands in her hair, tangling its strands, and shivers on her skin. Dragging down her back, her shirt torn from her shoulders. His fingers biting suddenly into her flesh. Sharpened nails, slicing in. Her body tearing with her clothes.

A single drop of blood fell from the corner of her mouth where it pressed against his, trickling down her chin.

She pressed herself against him all the harder.

He changed midway through her kiss. She had known he must. The semblance of man must fall away and it left only darkness, something rough under her hands. Something dripping red, inhuman and clutching. Claws ripping flesh, sharp points of teeth biting into her body. The reality of him came in flashes, too much to comprehend in total. She did not care. She embraced it. She wrapped her legs around it and cried out to the night.

She screamed, in the last. It was impossible not to. But she held on and got what she wanted.

#

In the night, the town sleeps with a sense of relief, if made unquiet with guilt. It was done, what had to be done. Sacrifice made, it would be enough.

It must be enough.

Behind locked doors, children lie safe, tucked in bed. They are watched by nervous parents reluctant to admit the snaking bead of doubt. Adults telling each other they did only what was necessary.

They only want to save the children.

Outside, all is quiet. The occasional torch flickers, shadows dance. In the stillness, a cat skittles away. A dog ducks its tail and runs to hide.

A woman stands at the edge of town. She is dressed in

flowing white and her skin is the same shade. Her eyes are only black. Beneath the hem of her dress, her feet are bare, with one pale ankle ringed a stark blue. A bruise, perhaps a scar. Perhaps a memory. A breeze rises up with her arrival, bringing an echoing cry, don't do this! Your children will not be safe! She drifts forward, dress billowing behind, black hair tangled like the woods from which she has come. There is blood at her lips. It stains her mouth, contrasts against the pallor of her skin.

Skin of snow, lips of blood, hair black as the darkness.

Behind locked doors, sleeping children toss in nightmare. The young who cannot know what their adults have done. She can feel the anxiety of parents. The desperation of the town. All their unspoken needs. Their fears. Their wants.

She wants.

The children. Sacrificed to save their children. Made to suffer for their children.

She wants to return that suffering. She wants them to scream. For the children.

The breeze picks up, brings its echoes. If there is a monster in these woods, it will take them...

She grins a bloodied, sharp-toothed grin and walks into the town.

The monster in the woods. Come to take their children.

ROAD TRIP
Anthony Ferguson

Richie shot Frankie a glance as his companion punched the keys on his mobile. He gripped the steering wheel hard. He could tell by the way Frankie was bouncing around in his seat that he was agitated. Richie didn't like it when Frankie got upset.

Nobody liked it when Frankie got upset.

'Christ's sake!' Frankie shouted and smacked the phone against the dashboard. 'How d'ya get a fucken signal in this godforsaken shithole?'

He held the phone out of the Commodore's passenger side window and shook it vigorously.

'Where the hell are we anyway?' he said over his shoulder.

'We're just outside of Manjimup, on the way to Bridgetown,' Richie said.

'How long 'til we get back to Freo?'

Richie chewed his lower lip. Frankie knew how long it would take. He had driven the reverse journey three days earlier. 'About three hours.'

Frankie flung the mobile over his shoulder and onto the back seat via the roof of the sedan. Richie braced himself for the onslaught.

'I've had it with these inbred hicks and their redneck shitholes. Ya can't get a phone signal, ya can't get the Internet, everything's overpriced and ya can't get good service. That's when the shops are even open. Christ, ya can't even get friggin' Italian food out here. Only bloody restaurants are Chinko, and who runs those? Not the bloody Chinese.'

Richie smiled. 'Christ, here we go.' He watched Frankie's Adam's apple jiggle up and down with agitation before the tirade resumed.

'How 'bout that joint the other night, eh? What's in the Chinese Hotpot I asked that ranga waitress, and what did she say? Aw oi dunno, Choinese shtuff. What the fuck is Chinese stuff? What's wrong with a bit o' spag bol? And I'm jack of payin' fifteen bucks fer a sandwich too. Nup, ya can stick ya friggin' country as far as I'm concerned.'

'Well, at least we got the job done with no hassles, took out Jimmy the Bull, like Enzo wanted.' Richie looked across for acknowledgement as he slowed to accommodate the vehicle ahead of them.

Frankie plucked a mint out of the packet sitting in the central console and stuck it in his mouth. Richie pictured the dissolving peppermint soothing his rage.

'Yeah, ya did okay on that one, Rich. Ya coming on good. I schooled ya well.'

'How many hits is that for you now, Frank?' Richie asked, trying to shift the conversation onto safer ground.

Frankie's brow furrowed. 'Let's see, that makes... thirteen now.'

Richie whistled.

'Yeah, what can I say? It's a living,' Frankie mused.

Richie gripped the wheel and stared at the chassis of the

old pick-up truck in front of them. A tentative sun peered through a crack in the gunmetal clouds and shed its light on the road ahead. Even Frankie conceded the south-west was gorgeous this time of year. The rains had created a fertile paradise among the fields and forests, and they had lapped up what little sightseeing their journey afforded them.

Richie hadn't known if he would be able to hack it when Enzo first brought him into the fold, but they threw him in the deep end and he had done whatever the Family asked. It was like Frankie said, 'When you're a wop and you're stuff all good at anything else, whaddya do? Ya join the Mob.' Having family connections helped, and when you're Italian, everybody's family. Even third generation bums like him and Frankie.

'What's this prick doing?' Frankie motioned toward the truck ahead as they rode its bumper. 'Bloody speed limit's a hundred and ten and he's sittin' on eighty.'

'Yeah, I know.'

'Can't ya overtake the dickhead?'

Richie waved a hand over the bitumen vista filling the windscreen. 'Well, I can't go over the double white lines, too many sharp bends on the road.'

Frankie lost it. 'Shit! You can shoot a bloke in the head but ya can't pass on a double line?'

'Take it easy. There's a passing lane coming up. We'll take him then.'

Frankie pulled the sunshade down and checked his reflection in the mirror. He adjusted the crotch of his jeans. 'Geez, I'm lookin' forward to gettin' home, eh? Gonna give the missus a bloody good seeing to.'

'Yeah?' Richie feigned interest. He cranked his window down a little to let the wind run through his hair.

'You still seeing that Saskia chick?'

'Nup. We broke up yonks ago.'

'Oh, that's right. She was two-timing ya, hey?' Frankie shook his head. 'Any bitch did that to me, I'd rub her out.'

'Angelica wouldn't do that to you, Frank. She's not that type of girl.'

'Oh, yeah? Know her that well, do ya, mate?'

Richie felt Frankie's eyes on him.

'No, of course not. It's just... You been married three years, you got a kid — Hey, we're coming up to Palgarup. We can lose this prick.'

The car descended into the town. As they rolled down the main street, Frankie spat the mint out the window. 'Hey, pull up here, mate. I'm starving.'

Two beef and mushroom pies and a ham and salad roll later, they were back on the road.

Frankie had his mobile again and was fighting to get a signal. Richie kept his eye on the road while his tongue probed a crack in one of his upper cuspids for a stubborn sliver of onion. At the same time, he replayed their earlier conversation for clues. Was Frankie prodding him for information back there? Nah, he's not that smart. Besides, everybody knows you don't cut someone's grass in the Family. Not if you want to keep your balls.

'Shit!' said Richie.

Frankie looked up from his phone. 'Fucken country hick!'

178

He reached across Richie's lap and leaned on the horn, then sprang back and stuck his head out the window. 'Hey, dickhead! Get outta the bloody way.'

'Unbelievable,' said Richie.

'Wait a minute. Isn't that the same prick who was holding us up before we got into Palgarup? Faded red pick-up? He should be bloody miles away by now.'

As if in response, the pick-up slowed down. An intermittent stream of traffic sped in the opposite direction.

'I don't believe this arsehole. Is this some sort of joke?' Frankie squeezed the mobile in his fist as if he wanted to crush it.

'Thank Christ.' Richie heaved a sigh as he hit the accelerator and pulled into the overtaking lane and passed the slower vehicle.

Frankie leaned out the window to give the guy a mouthful as they drew level and the truck accelerated ahead of them.

'What the...?'

The passing lane narrowed into nothing and the pick-up was waiting for them, as impassable as ever.

Frankie said. 'This guy is taking the piss. That's it.'

Richie swallowed. 'What's it?'

Frankie glanced over his shoulder toward the boot of the car. 'I'm taking this guy out.'

'Frankie, we ain't got time for this. Besides, we're on the open road, too many witnesses.'

The truck ahead of them indicated a left turn, even though there was no road to divert onto.

'Now what?' said Frankie.

Several minutes later, a side road came into view. The truck slowed to a complete stop at the junction, its indicator still flashing.

Richie said. 'What is he doing?'

Frankie broke into a smile. 'The dumb prick wants us to follow. We'll give him what he wants.'

Richie hesitated. 'What if it's a trap?'

'Nobody would go to that much trouble. Look at the guy. He's on his own. Enzo doesn't have any enemies out here, none that are still breathing anyway. He woulda warned us.'

The red pick-up eased around the corner and the white Commodore followed. A green road sign indicated the destination and the distance.

'Donnelly River. You know that place, Rich?'

'Nup. Never heard of it.'

'I know it, been there before. Keep going. We'll teach this wanker to mess with us.'

The road narrowed into a single lane, with orange gravel framing each side. Dense forest hemmed them in. Richie wandered over the middle of the tarmac and glanced up at the sun as it began its descent toward the horizon. 'Hope this don't take too long. It gets dark quick this time of year.'

'Yeah, don't worry. This guy ain't got long to live. Anything coming the other way will take him out before it gets to us. Just watch out for roos. They like to hit the paddocks around dusk.'

Half an hour later, the pick-up slowed and rounded a sharp bend. They followed until it rolled down a slope and came to a stop by a crumbling wooden structure.

'Woah! What the hell is that?' said Richie.

'It's the old wood pulping mill. Don't follow him, go up this way. He ain't going nowhere. It's the end of the road.'

Frankie guided them into a clearing by an abandoned cluster of stone buildings. They got out of the car and looked down the hill at the foreboding relic where the truck had parked. The decrepit mill was dank and dark and it had collapsed in places.

'That place looks haunted,' said Richie, wrapping his arms around himself to ward off the afternoon chill. He swore the cold was emanating from the rotting hulk itself, rather than the river beyond it.

'I bet it is. Lotta accidents happened there, from what I remember. Lotta accidents happened after it closed too.' Frank smiled.

'Whaddya mean?'

'Funny that guy leading us here. I did my first hit here, five years ago, right over there where he's parked, as a matter of fact. Small world, eh?'

Frankie popped the trunk and rummaged in a leather carry-all, retrieved a snub-nosed Glock.

'Should I bring my gun too, Frank?' Richie asked.

'Nah, mate. Leave this one to me.' Frankie slammed the boot of the car.

They walked past the crumbing main building and Richie's attention was drawn to a large noticeboard, hammered into the ground.

Frankie checked the gun's chamber. 'This used to be a bit of a tourist spot back in the day, but all that died out yonks ago. People stopped coming here. The ones living here left.'

Richie read from the noticeboard. 'Do not dwell in this sad place, where the dark ones watch from the shadows. What do ya suppose that means, Frankie?'

Frankie fitted a silencer onto the pistol. 'Stuffed if I know. Never saw it before.'

'Says it's a quote from an Abo elder. Not a very touristy message, is it?'

Frankie ignored him, staring dead ahead. 'I brought Angelica out here once.'

Richie flinched.

'Screwed her right over there, up against the wall. She likes it out in the open, but you'd know that, wouldn't ya Richie?'

'Frank...?'

Frankie turned toward him. 'Nah, don't say anything, mate. Just start walking.' He motioned toward the red pick-up.

'Aw shit. Come on, Frank.'

Frankie spoke with quiet authority. 'Shut up, Richie. Turn around. Don't even look at me.' Richie felt the barrel of the pistol pressing into his back.

Richie staggered ahead of his mentor. Down by the old mill, the occupant of the truck had alighted and stood with his back to them, staring out toward the river.

'I'm disappointed in you, Richie. I taught you the ropes, and this is how you repay me, by banging me missus.'

Richie wheeled around and dropped to his knees.

'I'm fucken sorry, Frank, all right? I'm sorry. Please don't do this. Don't let a woman come between us. It was her fault mate. She forced herself on me.'

'Don't make a spectacle of yourself, Richie. Try and act like a professional. We're hit men, fer Chrissakes. We got a job to do here, remember? There's no use arguing. I'm gonna do him and then I'll do you. Two birds with one stone. So get up and keep walking.'

Richie rose with the enthusiasm of a condemned man. He turned and placed one foot in front of the other. 'Please, Frankie...'

'The only question left, Richie, is whether you get it in the head or in the balls. Now move!'

A chill wind swirled up from the river as they approached their target and Richie noticed the silence which enveloped the area. There were no bird or insect noises, not even the sound of ebbing water. The man stood with his back to them, his hands in his jacket pockets. He was tall and angular, and dressed head to toe in black garb.

Frankie let out a bitter laugh. 'Turned out quite convenient this, eh, Rich? Enzo insisted I bring you back home to face the music, but now I figure, stuff that. Had a bit of trouble with a guy, he took Richie out before I could get him. Sorry, Enzo, but it's the nature of the business.'

Richie shivered and his teeth chattered. 'I don't like this place, Frank. We shouldn't have come here.'

'What are you scared of Rich, the mill? It's just an old building, you dumb shit.' Frankie shrugged his shoulders. 'If there are any ghosts, you'll be joining them soon. You can all haunt me together.'

Richie cast a sideways glance at the crumbling pulp mill.

It felt even colder up close, like it was sucking the life out of the air itself. He didn't like the way it made him feel like he was being watched.

As they neared the truck, Frankie stopped several metres from the motionless figure and shoved Richie aside. 'Hey... hey, arsehole! Turn around, so I can shoot you in the face.'

The man turned to face them. Richie dropped to his knees for the second time. Frankie's jaw hung slack.

'Shit!'

The visage staring back at Frank was that of the man he had executed five years before. At least, it was at first. Though it was difficult to tell for sure in the dull afternoon light, the face seemed to exist in a state of flux. First angular with a wispy moustache, then pear-shaped and clean-shaven, then fat and double-chinned. Calabrian, Sicilian, it mimicked the variation of human facial structures, but always in perpetual motion.

'Nooo!' Frank screamed. He backed away as the shadowy figure closed the gap between them with uncanny speed. Frank fired point-blank once, twice, a third time. The bullets smacked into the man's face, which seemed to open up and swallow them within its fleshy folds. Strong, wiry fingers closed around Frankie's neck, and he stared into the dead eyes of his victims, one after another. The Glock fell into the dirt.

'Richie...' he gasped.

Kneeling in the mud, Richie saw Frank's eyes bulging.

'Richie... help meee!'

Richie saw the gun lying at the feet of the two figures, but thought better of it. Frankie let out a keening whine as one of the hands moved from his throat and crept up his face. Richie stood transfixed as two of the fingers dug into Frankie's eye sockets and squeezed. Richie heard a sound like a boot crushing a blowfish and saw a stream of viscera ooze between those skeletal fingers. Frankie bellowed in pain.

Then Richie was running, pounding the dirt. He ran toward the river. He looked back to see the thing drop Frankie and point a long bony finger straight at him. Its eyes seemed to glow. Richie saw the car sitting on the hill beyond the outstretched arm. Then he turned and fled into the bush.

He tore through thick foliage which grabbed at him like gnarled fingers, and splashed along the shallows, not daring to look back. After a while, he slowed and stood, hands on his knees, panting. He listened for any sound, but the world was dead and silent. He hurried on, moving as far away from that awful scene as possible.

As he ran, he played scenarios out in his head. Frankie knew about him and Angelica, Enzo did as well. That meant that the Mob would have already whacked her. Christ, what was he thinking, crossing the Family? He couldn't go back, ever. He needed transportation. He should double back to the car. Then he would have wheels and a gun. He'd rather face the Mob than that thing back there. Maybe it only wanted Frankie. Maybe it had gone now. But it had pointed right at him. Christ!

Richie slowed to a walk. He looked around, trying to get his bearings. He could hear the river somewhere in front of him. It was pitch black, no moonlight filtered through the clouds. There was no sound of movement from the forest. He was sure that thing was not chasing him. He allowed a flicker of hope to penetrate his despair. If he could find the river and follow it, maybe he could retrace his steps, get to the car, even if it meant going past that mill again. It seemed the best option.

If only there were light to guide him. Then, as if in answer to his prayers, he saw a shimmer through the branches. It flickered in the night sky, like a million tiny lights being switched on.

'Stars,' he said.

Richie felt a surge of relief. He could use the stars to navigate his path out of the bush.

He moved toward the sound of the flowing water and focused on the stars. They shone like spun gold through the canopy, seeming to form patterns. Then Richie stopped in his tracks, his heart hammering. He saw the dark edifice of the mill loom before him. He spun in a circle as the glittering orbs encroached upon him from all sides, and realised too late that they were not stars at all.

BLOODLUST
Steve Cameron

I was checking in at reception when I felt the presence of someone standing close behind me. Not waiting for the clerk, waiting for me. White flowers sat in a tall jade vase on the counter. I closed my weary eyes for a moment, relishing the cool fragrant air and trying to imagine who it could be. I decided I'd let them make the first move, and opened my eyes once more. The clerk smiled, passed me my card and key, and I slipped them into my wallet. Grabbing my shoulder bag, I turned to leave without so much as a glance behind me.

'Toby McAllister.' A statement, not a question.

I stopped and turned around. The speaker was a rotund middle-aged Chinese man. Medium height, short thick hair, thin lips. He wore an expensive grey suit, but most importantly, he was holding out his police identification.

'Malaysian Police. I'm Inspector Chim,' he said, and gestured toward the lobby bar. 'Please, if I could have a moment of your time.'

'What's this all about?' I asked.

He gestured to the bar once more. 'Please.'

I sighed. 'Inspector, I've just flown in from Melbourne. I'm hot and tired and need a shower.' I paused. 'If it's not urgent, you can see me tomorrow. Otherwise, please just tell me what this is about.'

He shrugged. 'OK, Mr McAllister. Your life is in danger.'

Needless to say, we went to the bar.

\#

We sat opposite each other on leather couches, between us sprawled a low table. The Inspector drank a scotch while I sipped a pinot gris.

'You're not what I imagined, Mr McAllister. You don't look like a private detective.'

Which is true, I don't. I'm thirty-seven, but regularly pass as ten years younger. I'm medium height, quite slim, and have short wavy blond hair. My eyes are blue and I have a face that an ex-girlfriend once described as 'pleasing', whatever that means.

'So why is my life in danger, Inspector Chim?' I took a sip of my wine.

'I'm not going to beat around the bush. I know all about you. We need to trust each other here. We need to commence this conversation from the same point of reference.'

'Which is?'

'Vampires.' He smiled, and leaned back as though savouring a victory. My eyebrows lifted in surprise, not at the existence of vampires but that Chim knew about my involvement with the clans.

'Vampires,' I repeated.

He flipped open a small notebook and read. 'Twelve years with Victoria Police, including time in the Homicide squad. Six years as a private detective. Last year you did some work on Victor Wallace, the head of the Melbourne clan. Now you

188

take cases which, shall we say, have a paranormal element.'

'You have done your homework. Where did you get all this information from?'

'I have friends in Melbourne, Mr McAllister. I lived there for three years and did my undergraduate at Deakin University.'

'OK,' I said. 'Vampires, Melbourne, Victor Wallace. Why would my life be in danger here in Kuala Lumpur?'

He dropped his notebook back into his jacket pocket. 'Roland Lee. Mean anything to you?'

'Sure.' I frowned. 'I remember Roland Lee. I ran across him last year. He was an Australian-Chinese vampire who got bloodlust. The clan prefers to remain hidden nowadays, but he was bringing them unwanted attention. Rather than be discreet by having the occasional light feed, he returned to the old ways and ripped out a couple of throats before he was taken care of.'

'By you?'

'No,' I said. 'I'm an investigator, not a killer. He was staked by federal agents. I was there at the time though.'

'Not a killer? Not even of vampires?'

'Not even of vampires,' I said.

'That's not how the story was told here, Mr McAllister. Roland's cousin, Jimmy, is a hot-headed young vampire. He believes you're responsible.' He paused. 'And I have received intelligence he knows you're here and wants his revenge.'

#

189

The elevator foyer was shiny, all mirrors and glass. Chim and I were reflected on ten different surfaces, in ten different ways. Two pale girls, determined and confident, strode past. Blonde in a purple satin jumpsuit, brunette in a tight red miniskirt. Their heels clacked on the tiled floor. Barely out of their teens. Gorgeous, I thought.

'Russian hookers,' snorted Chim.

There was a soft chime and the doors swished open. 'I'll get changed and be back soon,' I said.

He nodded.

#

Chim seemed like a decent guy, so I took him up on his dinner offer. As we stepped out of the hotel onto the apron, the day's remnant heat slapped me and I suddenly felt very weary. The street was busy, traffic at a standstill in a darkening canyon of neon and illuminated signs. Ten-metre-tall models gazed at us from department store billboards. *Love awesomely*, declared one. *Celebrate the auspicious*, screamed another in large, gaudy letters. Chim's car arrived and we clambered into the back where it was cool and comfortable. The driver eased out into the traffic, and we sat in silence. I gazed out the window at the crowded footpaths as the traffic stopped and started, stopped and started. Mothers in hijabs and niqabs watched impassively as their children scampered ahead of them. Young women on mobile phones tottered past while herds of men in suits watched them with longing. Teenagers laughed and took photos of each other and themselves. The City Centre complex of plazas and malls was a shifting mosaic of colour and activity. Kuala Lumpur came alive in the cool of the evening.

'Walking through the KLCC underpass would have been faster,' I said.

Chim said nothing.

Finally, after a couple of right turns through easier traffic, we pulled up outside a chrome and glass skyscraper. I stared for a moment at the Petronas Towers which dominated the skyline, brightly illuminated against the dark sky like a photographic negative. They were so close I felt I could almost reach out and touch them. Chim ignored me and walked through the revolving doors into the building. I had to scamper to catch him.

Midnight Monsoon was on the fifteenth floor. The restaurant was quite full, and I could hear the gentle murmur of conversing couples. The maître d' said nothing as we entered, then nodded and guided us to a table, white tablecloth, silver cutlery and flickering candle in the low light. The night view of the ghostly towers filled the window alongside us. As we sat, Chim and the maître d' conversed in Chinese before departing. Chim was obviously a regular.

'I took the liberty of ordering wine for us both,' he said. 'I hope you don't mind.'

'That's fine.'

'So what's the fascination with Malaysia? You come here often.'

'About once a year on holiday,' I conceded. 'I first visited with my parents when I was young, and I fell in love with the place. I can relax here; forget about my workload for a week

191

or two. I enjoy the food, the culture, and I like the people.' I shrugged. 'I have an old friend here. I'm catching up with her tomorrow night.'

Inspector Chim's eyes narrowed, and he opened his mouth to say something. But he quickly closed it and stood as we were joined by an elderly Chinese man armed with a bottle of wine.

'Mr Fong, good to see you again,' said Chim. 'This is Mr McAllister, from Australia.'

I stood also, and thrust out my hand. Mr Fong smiled, and put down the bottle. Then he clasped mine and we shook.

'Sorry about the cold hand,' he said. 'I've just been out in the cool room sorting wine.'

I smiled. 'Come now, Mr Fong. I'm not stupid. How long have you been undead?'

Fong glanced at Chim. 'He's quick, this one.' He chuckled, then turned back to me. 'I've been undead for a hundred and thirty-seven years. I'm the chief of the KL clan. I hear Jimmy Lee is looking for you.'

'So I've been told. You do realise I had nothing to do with his cousin's death.'

'May I?' said Fong, and he indicated the third seat at the table. We all sat. 'It doesn't matter what I believe,' he answered. 'Jimmy believes it, and there's no way to convince him otherwise.'

'Can't you take care of him?' I asked.

'Jimmy has the bloodlust. He's out of control and won't acquiesce to our authority. He's formed his own faction, along with a few dim-witted followers. I have spread the word to leave you alone, but I fear it will be to no avail.' Fong opened the wine, poured three glasses, and said, 'It's on the house.'

I raised my glass, as did Chim and Fong, and we all drank.

'In Melbourne, the clan chief, Victor Wallace, takes care of those who get the bloodlust.'

'We would if we could.' Fong spread his hands. 'But he's gone underground. We're searching for him, but I fear he will find you before we can find him. We don't want to attract unnecessary attention to ourselves, but if anything happened to you, there could be an international incident.'

'And that would bring attention to the Clan from my government,' offered Chim.

'Exactly,' said Fong. 'May I suggest you return home as soon as possible? I'm sure the good inspector would pass a message to you once it was safe for you to return to KL.'

I shook my head. 'I'm not going to run just because a vampire threatens me. I work among the clans in Melbourne. My job would be nigh on impossible should they hear I ran from Jimmy Lee. I have a reputation to maintain.'

'An attitude that may see you killed. Very well, Mr McAllister. I wish you luck, and I will do what I can,' said Fong. He stood. 'May I recommend the sirloin steak? The chef selected them this morning.' He shook both our hands and departed.

'Steak?' I said to Chim as we sat.

He nodded. 'Midnight Monsoon has the best western cuisine in KL.'

'I'm on vacation. I was hoping for Malaysian.'

He shrugged. 'It's my money, my choice. But call Mr

Fong back if you want. Perhaps he can ask his chef to pour some satay sauce over it for you.'

#

My footsteps echoed along the underground passage as I walked through KLCC on my way back to my hotel in Bukit Bintang. I could hear the laughter of girls coming from ahead of me, but I could not see them or anyone else. The lights reflected off the tiled floors, while the murals and advertising on the walls stretched into the distance. Although Chim had insisted I be driven home, I had refused. I needed to stretch my legs, to clear my head and to think.

I could not believe Jimmy Lee was ready to kill me for something I had not done. I could not even imagine why he thought I was even involved. No one at home questioned the death of Roland. None of the clan in Melbourne harboured any grudge. Yet here I was, and the KL underworld thought me a killer.

There was no doubt Roland deserved to die. His bloodlust had caused the violent deaths of three people, three innocents. He had turned feral, and was out of control.

No, he had had to die.

But I was a detective, an investigator, not a killer. Even as a cop, I had loathed carrying a firearm. And when I made detective, I had pretty much stopped arming myself altogether. My echoed footfalls continued, the only sound in the passageway. I suddenly realised I could no longer hear the girls' laughter. I stopped, and took a breath. It was quiet,

194

unnaturally so. Slowly I turned, and fifteen metres behind me stood a tall man wearing sunglasses and dressed in black. Black pants, shirt and leather overcoat. His shoulder-length hair was swept back.

'McAllister,' he called softly.

'Jimmy Lee,' I said in response. 'I didn't kill Roland, if that's what you think.'

He shook his head slowly from side to side, tutting as he did so. 'McAllister, is that the best you can do? We both know you killed Roland. We both know you must die!' And with that, he screamed in rage and started running toward me.

I turned. I ran. I had no weapon, and I could hear the rhythmic pounding of his boots on the tiled floor. I pumped my legs as hard as I could. My arms flashing, my heart beating, my breath heavy. I quickly looked over my shoulder and saw that he was closer. He ran effortlessly, as vampires can. Ahead, in the distance, I could see the exit I needed. But I still had to reach it. And then I had to climb the stairs. And then I had to lose myself in a throng of people. And with each step, Jimmy was getting closer.

One foot after the other, I kept running. I almost slipped as my foot hit a patch of water, but somehow I managed to remain upright. Another glance. He was closer still, only five metres or so behind me. He screamed once more, a scream that made the hair stand up on the back of my neck. I pushed my legs to run faster, but they were going as quickly as they could. Just ahead, I saw an exit to the left. It wasn't the one for Bukit Bintang, and I had no idea where it emerged. Would it lead me into a crowd of shoppers where I might seek safety, or would it end in a dark alleyway where I would be trapped and have no chance of surviving? I decided to continue running to the exit I was familiar with. He was closer now, real close, and I fancied I could feel his breath on my neck — although this was surely just my imagination. As I ran past the exit on my left, I noticed two shadows step into the main tunnel. For a moment, I considered screaming at them, telling them to run before they got hurt. But it was me that Jimmy wanted, and while he was on my tail, he wouldn't pause to hurt innocents. Stopping would only ensure my death.

With every step, I waited for his hand to grab my neck, his nails to rip my flesh. He would then drag me down and hold me, his fangs slowly extending before he'd lean in and sink his teeth into me like a rabid animal. I risked a glance behind me once more, and shuddered to an abrupt halt. I was shocked to see two men in dark suits standing side by side, their backs to me and wooden stakes held high. On the far side of them, Jimmy paced savagely.

'McAllister!' he screamed at me. 'You're safe for now, but my time will come and you won't be able to escape for ever.' Then he turned and ran, his feet pounding along the tiled floor, and he was soon gone.

I bent double, dropping my hands to my knees, gasping for air and drenched in sweat. A moment later, I looked up and I was alone. The shadowy figures had also disappeared.

#

I slept until almost eight the next morning. For a while, I lay in bed, pondering the previous evening's events. I was lucky to be alive, of that I had no doubt. If it hadn't been for those two shadowy figures, Jimmy would have ripped out my throat and I'd have bled to death alone on the cool tiles. Had Inspector Chim assigned them to watch and protect me? Had it simply been luck? Were they simply a couple of anti-vampire vigilantes who lurked in dark places? Been in the right place at the right time. These vigilantes certainly existed in Melbourne, although the majority of people knew nothing of the undead in the midst of their community.

Finally, I got out of bed and took a shower. I allowed the hot water to play over my back and on my aching muscles. Although I worked out several times a week and jogged daily, my legs were still stiff from the previous night's run. I finished up, dried myself and dressed.

Daylight flooded into the room as I pulled back the curtains and opened the sliding door. The sound of traffic below met my ears. I closed my eyes and enjoyed the breeze that brushed my face. A moment later, I opened them and focused on a slash of purple on the balcony.

Inspector Chim had given me his business card the night before. I found it in my wallet, grabbed the phone and dialled.

'Inspector,' I said once he'd answered. 'Remember those Russian hookers last night? One of them is lying on my balcony with her throat torn out.'

#

Inspector Chim arrived a short time later with an Indian

197

assistant. I told him about Jimmy Lee chasing me and my unknown benefactors. He nodded and smiled.

'I know,' he said. 'I instructed those two officers to follow you.'

I frowned. 'Why didn't they grab Jimmy? They had their chance.'

'Mr McAllister,' he said. 'Their priority was to protect you, which they did. Once you were safe from harm, and Jimmy Lee turned to run, they indeed pursued him.'

'And?'

'And he got away. Vampires are quite fast, as you well know.'

We talked a little more about Jimmy, then he told me to find something else to do for a few hours. He'd organise a team to come and take the girl away and to clean up. Once they were done, he'd call me.

'Do you think Jimmy Lee is trying to set me up for this killing?' I asked.

'No,' he replied. 'That's not how he operates. He's letting you know you can't hide from him; that he knows where you are and he can get to you anytime he wants.'

'Not if I don't invite him in,' I said.

'He knows he can't get you in your hotel room,' said Chim. 'He's just trying to intimidate you.'

As I left, two more officers arrived; both dressed in telephone company overalls.

'It will attract less attention,' Chim told me.

'How will telephone maintenance men get a dead woman out without anyone seeing her?' I asked, but Chim told me not to worry. It would be taken care of.

I took a taxi out to the Islamic Arts Museum. The driver asked me where I was from, what I did for a living, whether I was married or not. I told him I was a maths teacher, which usually draws less interest than the truth. Instead, it caused him to ramble on non-stop, telling me about his daughter and the trouble she was having with her exams and how he and his wife were beyond despair. After that, the cool tranquillity of the museum was just what I needed. I wandered aimlessly for three hours, learning about Islam; the history, the culture and the art. Back outside was hot. The afternoon sun burned and I was relieved when the taxi back to KLCC was driven in silence.

I found a Starbucks, ordered an iced coffee and, with a copy of The New Straits Times in hand, sat under the slow ceiling fans. The park was full of young women and children chattering happily. Shoppers strolled past, arms laden with brightly coloured bags. There was no mention of any homicides in the paper. It seemed the recent killings by Jimmy were old news, or perhaps had not even made it to the media. I was sure the killing of the Russian hooker would also go unreported. I swirled my coffee and took another sip.

'Are you McAllister?'

I turned to see a young Malay boy on the other side of the café barriers. I nodded.

'Jimmy says he'll see you tonight. Don't be late.' And with that he turned and ran into the crowd of shoppers.

'Hey,' I shouted as I leaped to my feet. 'Hey!' I couldn't see him anymore. A couple at another table stared at me, disrupted by my shout. I sat back down and dialled Inspector Chim's mobile phone.

'I was just about to call you,' he said when he heard my voice. 'It's all clear. You can come back anytime.'

'I just had some kid run up and tell me Jimmy would see me tonight and not to be late. What's that about, do you suppose?'

Chim grunted. 'Kid was probably given a couple of ringgit to deliver the message. But it makes sense. There was a note addressed to you on the hooker's body. Do you know Pavilion?'

'Sure,' I said. I knew it well. The shopping mall was only a few hundred metres from my hotel.

'Jimmy says to meet him in the food court in the basement at midnight. Alone.'

'I'm not going. He's a vampire. He's stronger and faster. What makes him think I'd even consider going?'

'Mr McAllister. Do you know a woman named Felicity?'

It was hot, even under the fans, but my blood instantly froze as icy fingers ran up my spine. 'Yes,' I finally said. 'She's the friend I'm catching up with tonight.'

'Jimmy has her,' said Inspector Chim. 'And if you don't meet him at Pavilion, he says he will turn her.'

#

Felicity was a Malaysian student in my class at university. We became friends, then lovers for a short time, before realising we were better as friends. We stayed in touch and visited each other whenever we could. I had no idea how Jimmy could have learned of her existence, or my connection to her, but Jimmy had forced a showdown. I had no choice but to be in Pavilion's food court at midnight.

Inspector Chim was waiting for me in my room. Together, we attempted to formulate a plan, some way that I would be able to defeat Jimmy Lee. We discussed snipers, but bullets did no harm to a vampire. He suggested soldiers armed with stakes, martial arts experts, much like the two who had saved me in the underground passage. The problem, though, was that Jimmy held all the cards. We had no idea how far his network extended. We didn't know how many vampires would be with him, or what surveillance he had on the food court.

And he had Felicity.

One wrong move on my part and he could torture her in ways I could not even imagine. Once he was done with her, he could turn her and she would be gone, undead, and actually grateful for it.

Then he would still be free to come after me.

No. There was only one way, only one thing that would work. A tried and true method I had previously used. I told Inspector Chim what I needed. He said he would obtain it for me.

#

Inspector Chim had teams of officers waiting outside, discreetly covering all entrances. We had no way of knowing whether Jimmy was already inside, and if so, where he might be. He wished me luck, and I entered through a side door. Inside was dead quiet. I laughed at the irony, then made my way down the unmoving escalators. The food court was, of course, closed and empty. Chairs and tables had been wiped clean and smelled of industrial detergent and curries past.

'Jimmy,' I called out, and heard my voice echo back at me. I walked carefully, my hand clutching the illegal, high-powered stun gun in my pocket. It was already activated and ready to go. I would only have one shot, one chance to bring the vampire down. If I missed, I'd be dead before the stun gun could recharge. On my belt were the handcuffs I'd need once he was unconscious. Slipped into the waistband of my jeans was a stake. I'd taken it reluctantly, but only because Inspector Chim had pointed out that I'd need at least one weapon should the stun gun fail.

Slowly, I weaved my way between the tables, out toward the middle of the court. There was a kiosk there, and I cautiously checked Jimmy wasn't on top of it. I heard a rustle and a scrabbling sound, but could see no movement. My heartbeat thudded in my ears, and my hands grew clammy. Step by step, I made my way around the kiosk. At the far end, I saw a mannequin in bright yellow clothes. I frowned. It seemed to be set in the form of a crucifix, its arms outstretched and legs together.

Then it moved.

'Felicity,' I called out, and ran a few steps. She moved once more. I stopped when I heard Jimmy's laughter, and then he dropped out of the above darkness to stand a few metres in front of the bound woman.

'So,' he called out. 'You decided to come and play after all?'

'Let her go,' I replied. 'She means nothing to you. I'm the one you want.'

'Tempting,' he mocked. 'But I've grown quite attached to her these past few hours. And she does taste quite delightful.' He grinned, and then smacked his lips. 'So very delicious.'

'If you've harmed her...' I started walking slowly toward him.

'You'll what?' he interrupted. 'Arrest me? Send me to jail? Cry? Boo hoo hoo.' And then he threw back his head and laughed.

'Why, Jimmy? Why do you have to do this? Why do you have to kill? You could live like the others do. The occasional bite of a drunk, a quick nibble on a homeless person. The government turns a blind eye as long as you're discreet. I don't get it.'

'Why?' he roared. 'Why? Because it's our nature. That's why? You want me muzzled like some lapdog, like a tame puppy, denying my very nature, my very existence. That's not living. Look at the others. Even by our standards, they're dead inside. I want to live, to taste life, to be what I was meant to be.'

'I don't want to fight you. Just let Felicity go and we'll both leave quietly.' I glanced at her. She wore a tight yellow dress. Duct tape bound her hands and feet to a railing. A gag was firmly around her mouth.

'Nuh-uh,' he said. 'We're going to fight.' He grinned once more, and then launched himself at me.

I was about five metres away from him and he was getting closer. I tightened my grip on the stun gun. I felt like I'd been slammed by a runaway train when he hit me and I was forced onto the floor, unable to breathe. My fingers lost their grip on the stun gun, still in my pocket, and I struggled to stand. But he was on me again, wrestling me and laughing maniacally. He straddled me, knees to either side of my body, and one hand firmly holding my chest. My left arm flailed wildly and beat uselessly against his body. I snaked my right arm back toward my pocket. His right hand grasped my forehead and started to twist it, forcing my neck to stretch. He leaned in and I could smell the fetid stench of his mouth. My eyes widened as I saw his fangs move closer and closer. Then suddenly, he screamed in fury as I pressed the arcing stun gun against his leg. His back arched, and he struggled to keep hold of me. The charge only lasted five seconds and then it died. He still held me, although more loosely than before. I had fought to keep the electrodes pressed against him, but they must have lost contact. He had not been knocked unconscious, merely weakened. He continued to fight, hands scrabbling and scratching my skin as he tried to get a hold. I punched him and managed to roll him on his back. The longer this fight continued, the more my chances of winning decreased. He was regaining strength while I was weakening. I pushed myself up until I was sitting astride his chest. I pulled the stake from my waistband and raised it high. He stared at me, realising all was now lost.

'I didn't kill Roland,' I said.

'You're so full of shit,' he muttered. 'Fong told me you

did.' And then he died with a scream as I drove the stake into his heart.

#

It took me a moment to remember Felicity. I was spent, but I stood and raced to release her. She collapsed against me, crying in my arms.

'Are you all right?' I asked repeatedly, but she could only manage to nod between sobs.

'Mr McAllister.'

I looked across to see Inspector Chim and Mr Fong striding toward me. Behind them was a team of police and a couple of paramedics.

'Well done,' said Chim. 'You killed Jimmy and rescued the girl. Just like in the movies.'

I nodded.

The paramedics eased Felicity from me. I faced Chim and Fong.

'You bastard,' I said.

'I'm sorry?' he said coolly. 'I have no idea what you're talking about.'

'You knew. You knew I didn't kill Roland, yet you and Fong were the ones who made sure Jimmy heard it was me. Jimmy told me before he died. You also told him about Felicity. You're the only person who knew I had a friend here, and you told Jimmy.' I jabbed his chest with my finger. 'What was this? Some kind of war between factions of the clan? You wanted Jimmy gone but couldn't be responsible? I came along, and so you found your scapegoat, a fall guy to do your dirty work and take responsibility for it.'

Chim stared impassively.

'I was right. You are a quick one,' said Fong. 'But it all worked out, didn't it? The clan was on the verge of a civil war in KL. Jimmy had gone feral and was planning to revolt against us. If we'd taken care of Jimmy, his faction would have sought revenge. They're a close group, but without Jimmy to put thoughts in their heads, they'll be happy to toe the line. This way, peace is brought to KL.'

'All worked out? What in hell do you mean? Felicity is traumatised and we both could have been killed.'

'It would have been a small sacrifice for the greater good, don't you think, Mr McAllister?' Chim finally joined in the conversation. 'And if anything had happened to you, Jimmy would have been taken care of by us and we'd have said you'd managed to do it.'

'And Felicity?'

'We'll tell her she was kidnapped by an escaped psychopath. She wouldn't believe he was a vampire anyway. He wouldn't have harmed her. It was you he wanted.'

'Bullshit! He'd already tasted her. He was going to turn her.'

Chim shrugged, 'It doesn't matter. It all worked out. No real harm was done.'

'No,' I said. 'No harm was done. Except I can never return to KL because a faction of the clan now wants me dead.' I narrowed my eyes. 'All because you turned me into a killer, something I'm not.'

'He was already dead, Mr McAllister.'

'It doesn't matter,' I said. 'I'm no better than them now.' I turned, my fists clenched, and strode away.

ELFFINGERN
Dan Rabarts

Eins (1)

Smoke and blood. Mud and steel. The thunder of artillery, the chatter of machine guns, the grind of tanks.

Two brothers, pressed hard against the wet trench wall, panting. Rifles tight to their chests, dirt rattling on their helmets as they wait for a lull, wait for the order to throw themselves into the fury of the German machine gun nests.

One more breath, one breath too long. A shell lands with a roar a score of yards distant.

Two brothers, lifted and thrown sideways like little more than sacks of coal. The hollow ringing in the ears, the dull echo of screams, the hot burn of shrapnel. One brother, mouth agape but no sound coming out, staring at the burnt, bleeding stump of his elbow, his hand and forearm twitching in the mud several feet away. The other, staring through the hole in his left hand where his smallest finger had been, pulsing blood through burnt flesh. Too dazed, too numb for pain. He looks at his brother, not dead yet, but lying, gasping, bleeding. He ought to cry out for help, but here in the blinding madness of the trenches, of other men's war, so very far from home, there is no one to hear.

The touch of sudden snow drifting from smoke-wracked skies, settling on his ravaged hand, melting pink with his blood

208

and dripping into the earth. He imagines himself sinking into the earth, like dripping blood, melting snow, silent screams.

The crunch of boots in mud and debris, someone calmly approaching. The soldier looks up, gazes upon the figure standing head and shoulders above the top of the trench, and waits for the fool's head to explode in a burst of hot lead. The figure's coat is long and ragged, too smeared in mud and ash to identify insignia or rank. His battered helmet serves no better to identify him. The stranger crouches in the mud beside the dying brother, who gibbers like a lost babe. A bloody knife appears from inside his coat.

James watches as the apparition grabs his brother's remaining hand, and screams as the knife comes down.

Zwei (2)

'No,' Mary repeated, more firmly this time, as they crossed the garden between the parking lot and the sanatorium. 'The doctor's telegraph was very clear. We are not to talk about it. He finds it very upsetting.' She fussed with her black veil while the wind tried to snatch it away.

'I just want to know what it was like, mum. It must've been so exciting.'

'Eric, that's enough.' She swallowed the rest of her reply. He was only eleven, after all. He only knew what the newspapers told them, of glory and victory and heroes. Not of what that glory cost. It was little comfort that even though his father — a hero, apparently — would not be coming home from the war in Europe, Eric was brimming with excitement at the prospect of visiting his crippled uncle. Both had been gone a long time, especially for a boy growing up without a father.

Behind the stone monolith with its dozens of blind staring eyes, rows of pine trees swayed in the rising breeze, like a curtain to hold back the world. Mary shivered, and told herself that it was only the frigid wind. She couldn't afford a bad impression on this visit. Maybe the world was falling apart, but she still had a responsibility to provide for her son, by any means possible.

Beyond the tall doors lay the echoing corridors of the convalescent home. Mary wondered if she didn't prefer the gnawing of the wind without to the sterile chill within. Upon enquiry, a nurse escorted them toward the day room.

'He doesn't talk much,' she informed them. 'We get a lot coming through like that. He sits and watches the trees, mostly. Please don't talk about the war. It's likely to upset him, or those around him.'

Mary looked pointedly down at Eric, who jammed his hands into his pockets.

Uncle James sat in a soft-cushioned wheelchair, a blanket over his knees, staring out the full-length windows at the swaying pine trees marking the boundary of the hospital property. Beyond them, the dark of tree and bush, wet earth and shadow.

Mary lowered herself onto the overstuffed couch beside her brother-in-law, motioning for Eric to sit, and to his credit he did so. She and William had raised him to listen to his elders and do as he was told. Maybe it was the unnatural quiet, the vacant looks, but his natural vivacity was somewhat subdued.

Maybe the sight of his uncle in a wheelchair had made it all a little more real.

'Hello James,' Mary said, putting on her most genuine smile as she lifted the mourning veil from her face. 'We're so very pleased you're home.'

James stared past her, his gloved hands clasped in his lap.

'I see they gave you a medal,' Mary continued, determined. 'You must have been very brave.'

Mary felt a tug on her dress and turned to see Eric giving her his most darling frown. Just like that, she had broken the very rules she had set for him. Don't talk about the war. But what else was there to talk about? And if not to talk about it, how would they ever overcome what had happened there?

'James,' she said, 'your brother left a clause in his will that if he was to die and you were to survive him, that you are to inherit his stake in the printing business in Thames. There is...' She swallowed hard, and pressed on. 'I have made a room ready for you, so you will have a place to stay and a job when you're ready to work.'

James stared into the trees, into the darkness. 'Eric,' he said at last, his voice harsh as barbed wire, 'fetch me some water.'

Eric hurried away.

'James?' Mary urged him.

'I watched William die, Mary.'

Mary blinked away a sharp sting. Don't talk about the war. It may upset the soldiers. But what of the widows?

'James, I—'

The veteran's gloved hand snapped up and she fell silent.

James may have gone away to war a volunteer, a bookish lad filled with stories and hope, but he had returned as someone else. Stronger? Perhaps. Or was he now nothing more than dragon's teeth and shrapnel wrapped up in razor wire? 'Now you want me to come home with you.'

She heard what he did not say; that a war widow's pension was not money enough to raise a growing boy; that the years alone were more than she could face; that he remembered how he had once looked at her, when they were younger and his dashing older brother had been courting her, and how James with his awkward hands and shyness might never hope to dance with a young lady as fine as Mary; how in this world that the war had left behind, they must do the best they could with what broken pieces remained.

'It was in his will,' she repeated, wishing her veil might still conceal the flush in her cheeks. 'But you needn't feel obliged...'

James fixed her with a gaze which was all smoke and pain and the paling of dead flesh. One hand wrapped around the other as if to hide it, or to tear it off, if only he were able. 'I saw things, Mary, things I wish I had never seen. I had to... make choices.'

He turned away as a glass clanked onto the tray table and Eric took up his place on the couch, hands folded in his lap.

James met the boy's eyes, and nodded.

Drei (3)

The knife arcs up, and William screams.

The coated figure stands. James sees that its face is a bloody mess of exposed flesh and burnt skin, one eye leering sideways from a socket scoured of its eyelid. It lifts its prize — a single finger trailing a spool of blood — toward its mouth.

James jams the rifle against his shoulder and squeezes the trigger.

Black dust explodes from the ghast and it sways, but does not fall. It puts the bloody end of the finger into its mouth and sucks, as if inhaling on a fine cigar.

James can only watch as William gasps, twitches, and grows pale. A white vapour rises from his skin as his back arches, though whether in agony or rapture James cannot be sure. The white mist swirls toward the ghast, who continues to inhale, even as another shell explodes nearby, raining them with wet, hot debris.

William lies still. As the smoke clears, the monster is walking toward James, unhurried, unperturbed. Its face is no longer blasted but whole, yet somehow even more horrific for what James has just seen. The bloody knife hangs loose in its grasp as it approaches. James fumbles with his ruined hand to cock the rifle, but he is too slow.

Vier (4)

Mary fumbled for words which did not verge on desperation. Thankfully, James found them for her.

'He looks like his father, when we were lads.'

An age ago. Another world. Different men.

'That's what your mother always said.'

213

'Boy needs a man around.'

Somehow, it sounded no less desperate for having come from him, rather than her. Mary looked up with renewed hope. In his eyes, however, was not the warm paternal glow she craved. It was something she recognised all too well, something windblasted, wounded, and riddled with fear.

'We'd be so pleased,' Mary said, trying to sound cheerful and unafraid, choosing not to see the hollow, ravenous light in his eyes, or how James looked at Eric like a hunter sizing up his prey. She reminded herself of where he had been, what he had seen, what that must do to a man's heart. He wasn't William; William was never coming back. She and Eric needed James, no matter how broken, how bitter. Perhaps in time, she could make him well again, and he could learn to be as good a father as William had been. They may yet be able to salvage a future out of the ruins left behind by the war. There was enough ruin in this world that surely a woman ought not to be begrudged for trying to find a sliver of sunlight when the clouds broke, if only for a short time.

'I must heal,' James said finally, looking away.

'Of course,' Mary said, 'and your legs—'

'My legs are fine,' he snapped, causing Mary to flinch. 'I can walk. These doctors coddle me. I have other wounds which must be tended.' Slowly, deliberately, he eased the glove back from his left hand. It was loose, as if a size too big. Beneath it was a bandage seeping yellow and red, where two fingers should've been.

Mary tried not to gag as Eric sat forward, his face alight. The waft of charred flesh overwhelmed the antiseptic swill of

214

the hospital, carrying hints of mud, cordite, decay and, oddly, snow.

'We will change the dressing twice a day until it is healed. I trained as a nurse, remember.'

James replaced the glove, a smile twitching his lips as he studied Eric's rapt expression. 'It may heal in time,' James said, 'or it may not. We will see.'

Fünf (5)

James bunches his shoulder to thrust, ready to ram his bayonet through the approaching thing. He can barely grasp the rifle, his arm in agony, but desperation drives him on. It is one thing to fall in a hail of machine gun fire, but this is something else altogether. With a cry, he lunges, but the monster knocks him aside. For a moment, they grapple, among the dirt and the dead. James, his left hand a bloody mess, is outmatched, and the thing pins him down. He's on his knees in the mud, bent double, his wounded hand wrenched behind his back in a blossom of fresh agony. He hears steel slice through flesh, bone, and the distant sound of his own screams.

Tossed aside, he lies in the mud, clutching his bleeding hand to his chest, and listens to the squelch of boots. He weeps, a boy who wanted only to sit in a quiet patch of sunshine reading books, and waits to die. He has been waiting for this since the day he volunteered, but has only now come to realise its sheer, brutal inevitability. Through the haze of his tears, he sees a sticky thread of spooling blood, lacing patterns on the creature's mud-caked boots, drawing his eyes up to meet the monster's as it lifts James' finger to its lips.

'Shh,' it whispers, and laughs.

Sechs (6)

Wind groaned mournfully through the pines as Mary, James and Eric made their way along the lane to where the Ford was parked. An orderly carried James' duffle, the muzzle of a rifle protruding from it. He loaded it onto the car's rear platform while Mary helped James into the car.

As they drove, Eric finally had a chance to ask some of his most burning questions. James stared past the rain, and offered answers of one or two words, if any. Mary chose not to tell the boy to desist. The sooner they started down the road to casting out James' ghosts, the better.

It was almost dark when they arrived at the small cottage behind the press shop, the old pines along the hill groaning in the wind. Eric dutifully carried Uncle James' bag to the back room while Mary stoked the fire, filled the kettle, and dished plates of stew that she had put in the oven to cook before they had left that morning. She found James at the front step, wind gusting past him, gazing across the Hauraki Plains as curtains of rain stalked the horizon.

'Come sit by the fire,' she said, easing him inside and settling him on William's armchair near the potbelly. While she busied herself with the gas lamps, James' eyes drifted restlessly, settling on nothing.

Eric set the table, and so the evening progressed in an awkward parody of normality.

'Old Mister Lux has been helping run the shop since you left,' Mary told him, after Eric had gone to bed and she sat on a stool, unwinding the soiled bandages from James' hand. 'He's happy to show you the ropes, but he'll be just as happy to go back into retirement. He did it as a favour, keeping the place going these past couple of years.' The bandage peeled away, revealing a raw mass of flesh still red and black in places, oozing thin blood and pale yellow fluids. Why was it taking so long to heal?

James stared into the stove's emberous slivers. He had moved the chair — William's chair — ever so slightly, so it no longer faced into the room, but toward the fire. 'What do we print?'

Mary blinked. It was a strange, hollow question. James had lived all his life in this town, including the years that William had run the printing press. He knew what the press printed. 'What our customers want. Advertising, brochures and posters and the like, mainly.'

'No newspapers.'

Mary dropped the bandages into a bowl of water, the stain spreading. 'William's gazette—'

'No news stories, nothing political. And I don't want any newspapers delivered here.'

A chill fluttered in her stomach. 'James, the world goes on. The war is still—'

He slammed his good fist into the armchair. 'If not for the newspapers and the government and their lies, we never would've gone, Mary. William would still be here, and I wouldn't be living on your charity.'

In the stillness that followed, the only sounds were Eric's quiet cries from the next room. Mary set her bowl down and left James and his open wounds to the comfort of the flames.

Sieben (7)

The creature kneels in the mud before James tilts his chin with one cadaverous hand, so he must meet its eyes. In its other hand, it holds James' finger, congealing blood hanging like a tail from a sliver of bone. James looks into the creature's face, which is long, thin, too elfin to be human, its eyes pale and ancient as glacier ice. It is grinning.

'Meine', it says, and touches the dismembered digit to its thin, dry lips. It inhales sharply, and James shudders as burning cold drives into his chest. He gasps, a piece of himself freezing, breaking, severing away. His strength fades as his terror grows, and hot tears spill down his cheeks. Finally, something warm in this place which has been nothing but cold and rain and mud and snow for so very long. William is dead. There's no one to see him cry. No one to see his shame.

But he won't die like this, sucked dry by this spawn of dark German forests and the darker legends that grow there, a creature of twisted black boles and windshriek river canyons and nightmare. His good hand snakes inside the creature's coat, and he snatches one of its bone-handled daggers. The thing recoils in surprise, as James plunges the knife into his own chest.

218

Mary found Eric in the printing press, huddled over the assembly board in the ruddy glow of a single gas lamp. The machines sat silent around them.

'What are you writing?'

He looked up at her, his face drawn, older than it should have been. Tired. She glanced at the inverted letters he was so painstakingly setting on the plate, but they made no sense to her. His fingers and face were smudged with black ink, like William's had always been at the end of the day.

'Stories,' he said, looking away, embarrassed. 'Just silly stuff.'

'It's late. Uncle James wants to talk to you, about school.'

Eric drew back. 'He's not my dad.'

'We're not having this discussion again. Your uncle wants you to tell him about these stories, the ones you give out at school.'

'I don't give them away; I sell them, a penny each.'

'Let's talk inside. You're not in trouble, darling. Uncle James just has a few questions. He just wants to talk.'

'He never just wants to talk. He wants to make me feel small and worthless and horrible. That's all he ever does. He's a nasty man, and I don't like him.'

Mary flinched. Such vehemence, from one so young. Such brutal honesty. But even if Eric was right, she needed James, and her son needed to respect him. In time, that respect would be reciprocated, she was certain. But for now, Eric was the boy, and James was the man. 'You will do as you're told and come inside now.' She pointed to the door, where the last rays of evening light painted the timber frame in shades of fire and blood.

Eric stomped away from the small corner table which held the manual press, an anachronism enshrined. The small hand-driven press had been the start of William's business, embodying his youthful fascination and passion for print, which had evolved into a career and a livelihood. How terribly she missed his enthusiasm, his determination. He had always wanted to capture the world in black and white, with his weekly gazette featuring stories of success and celebration and local interest. Had he survived, how would he see this world now? In black and white? Or in shades of grey and red?

As Mary reached up to extinguish the gaslight, her eyes caught a single word on the offset plate mounted on the table. While she lacked William's knack of reading letters backwards, the single word isolated from the blocks of text above and below it, emphasised by italicised letters and quotation marks on either side, was almost impossible not to read. The single word, for all that it was foreign and stood out on the page devoid of context, sent a shiver through her, for reasons she could not express:

'Meine.'

Neun (9)

'Nein!'

The ghast lunges, its skin dry like old paper as it grips James' hand, hot with his pumping blood. James' severed finger falls forgotten into the mud as man and monster wrestle for the knife, for the right to claim the soldier's dying moments. James clutches the handle tight, determined to die by his own hand before the ghast can suck him dry. But it tears his fingers loose, and wrenches the blade free.

Still, his blood pulses down his muddy fatigues in an ever-weakening stream. James grimaces, savouring victory.

The ghast leans forward, a wicked gleam in its eyes like sun lancing off alpine peaks, and pushes its fingers inside his chest wound.

'Meine,' it says, through brittle teeth and bleeding gums. 'Du bist meine.'

Zehn (10)

'Where did you hear these stories?' James asked, waving one of the hand-pressed penny-dreadful sheets.

Eric shrugged. 'I make them up. They're just stories.'

James gave him a hard look. Mary wondered at his intent, but he remained so remote that she couldn't guess.

'You just think of them,' James said, his voice flat. 'These stories of ghosts and war and violence. From your eleven-year-old brain.'

Eric nodded.

James slapped the paper with his crippled hand. 'These stories don't even make sense. They're little more than... scraps of dreams. Why would anyone pay to read them?'

Eric shrugged, sinking further into himself. 'I guess they like them, Uncle. People like stories, stuff that isn't real.

Stories where bad stuff happens, but it's not happening to them.'

Mary frowned. This was not what she had expected of the conversation. So what of Eric's inspiration? What about his suffering schoolwork, and the hollow, haunted look in his eyes?

'Are you sure, Eric? For there is nothing entertaining about war, or death. Or is it that you have dreams? Bad dreams?'

Mary sat frozen as Eric turned his gaze to his uncle, and in the gaslight she saw moisture glistening in his eyes. She put a hand on his shoulder, but he recoiled from her touch.

'And what of this Elffingern you wrote of? Did you dream him, too?'

Eric paled, and nodded. When he spoke, his voice was a cracked whisper. 'Every night, uncle.'

Elf (11)

James gasps, his eyes flaring open, and the breath in his lungs burns cold as winter. Ice runs through his veins and the world is rimed in frost, and mist, the grey dirt of the trenches and the long pallid puddles all stripped of colour. But all he can see is the face before him, a leering mask of withered flesh peeling back from tooth and bone. The coat and helmet and knives are gone, leaving the creature almost naked in this colourless otherworld blanketed in the drifts of a Bavarian December. The ghast is clothed in string upon string of bones, short and thin — finger bones, all strung together with white knotted sinew.

The creature holds James, one hand wrapped around his

neck, one inside his chest, the cold pouring into his heart.

'You,' it hisses into his ear, 'are mine.'

James gags.

'Mine,' it breathes again. 'I am Elffingern, and you are my eleventh, as each before you has been my eleventh, and as each after you will be. They speak of me in frightened whispers, the widows and the children and the fearful, but with time, they forget, and stop believing. This is when I hunt, when the legend of Elffingern grows silent in the long dark memories of trees and in the songs of the little ones as they ring around their rosies, their pockets full of posies. I am he of the eleven fingers, and you will remember me, in the short falling of the hours and days you have left, and your nightmares will spill into the world, and there I will be. As long as I have...'

The monster pauses, as if realising that it has forgotten something. Realising it has grown vain and careless. It has made a mistake.

Its eyes dart sidewise, to where James' finger lies in the muck. It releases him and grabs for the severed digit.

James sucks in a breath and somehow, perhaps by the rush of human desperation, perhaps by the eternal light that burns for heroes in the dark depths of a fairy tale, finds the strength to strike. He snares the string of bones on Elffingern's chest and yanks. Something breaks, some part of the ghoul, or of the world.

Elffingern screams, and the trenches devolve into white. Through the collapsing swirl of light and ice and pain, James grinds out a single agonised word:

'Mine.'

Zwölf (12)

James put down the last sheet and folded his arms.

Mary had watched as James read the ten stories Eric had already written, just as she had watched as William had gone away to war, and as the world had gradually fallen to pieces around her. She was fading, a bystander, a ghost abandoned by the past. Her throat was tight as she looked at her son, withering under her brother-in-law's heartless gaze; the man she had hoped might one day warm her bed and brighten her mornings, like her William once had.

But she also wanted him to step in, to take charge, to make the hard choices. If she intervened at this critical point in their fledgling relationship, the opportunity would be lost. She would for ever be an interfering mother, a haven for Eric to flee to. The world had a way of sweeping such havens away. Eric must learn respect, must know his place, and accept that the world is harsh and unforgiving. This was James' chance to be that man. James, who had always lived in his brother's shadow. James, who had never been able to talk to the young ladies. He had always been slight and somewhat abashed, caught up in books until he got caught up in war and became a man before he was done with being a boy.

Now here they were, the widowed and the wounded, bound up in the fractured pieces left behind. Behind her, the two rifles which had served the brothers were mounted over the threshold in a crude salute, their barrels crossing. She missed William more than ever at that moment, but William wasn't coming home. So many were never coming home. James; dear,

224

sweet, shy James, was her best chance at happiness. She had to give him room to adjust, to find his own way through the minefield of fatherhood that they never offered pre-combat training for.

So lost was she in her thoughts that she was startled as the pair of them, man and boy, rose from their respective seats and headed for the door, for the settling gloom of night. She took a hesitant step after them. 'Where are you going?'

James turned, waving a penny in one gloved hand. 'I understand there is another story ready to go to press. I intend to purchase the first copy.'

Mary stood speechless, transfixed by the unexpected grin on Eric's face. She watched as they trooped off into the gloaming toward the print shop, like she had so often watched William trudge off into the pre-dawn shadows. She stood still, her mind racing, lifted by Eric's smile but equally haunted by the look she had seen in James' eyes. The same look she had seen in the sanatorium. The hunter, stalking.

No, she told herself. He's taking an interest. James has always been fond of stories, of books. He's merely taking up Eric's enthusiasm, finding a common ground. She allowed herself a nervous smile as the two figures, one tall and stooped, the other small and vulnerable, disappeared into the gloom, framed by the arc of trigger guards and rifle bolts. Mary tried not to let the sick feeling in her belly overcome her; tried not to dwell on that haunted, hungry gleam in James' eye.

She pushed the door closed, familiar with the clank that the two rifles made against each other as it shut. Whether James had hung them there in some pique of dark pride or as a constant reminder of the past, she didn't know. She would rather not see them, ever again. She would rather forget.

In the warm glow of the stove and the gaslight, Mary tried to take comfort in the hope that given time her house would become again a place of warmth and laughter. A place for her son to grow, and thrive, and create, like his father had. Like William would've wanted.

She looked at the papers now scattered on the occasional table beside William's — James' — armchair. Stories, inspired by nightmares. Her poor boy! What awful things were invading his sleep? Things he couldn't tell his mother, but couldn't bear to keep inside. She picked up the pile, sorted through to find what appeared to be the first in the sequence. Eric was as meticulous with dating his work as William always had been. She sat beneath a gaslight, and started to read.

Dreizehn (13)

The whiteout is clearing. James stands ankle-deep in snow. On all sides, as the blizzard lifts, he can see tall black trunks, misshapen boughs clawing the white sky. A trail of red drips leads into the dark places between the trees. James knows what he will find if he follows that trail, like breadcrumbs through the forest, and it won't be a gingerbread house. It will be a cave, or a hovel, or the cold innards of a tree grown too deep, too ancient to offer anything like sanctuary. It will be a lair, where Elffingern huddles, little more than dry skin stretched over bones too thin, too frail to give chase, too weak to fight. It will be cowering, the bloody trophy clutched to its ribs, its last remaining source of the vitality it needs to stay alive, to be needed, to not be forgotten. The last vestige of belief anyone might have of a lost spectre of folklore turned cold as ashes under the driven snow.

James looks at his own hands. One, shredded by shrapnel and butchered by fey steel, the other clutching tight to a grisly string of yellowing phalanges, each one a fragment of some poor soul, their strength the life-force that sustains the monster which has fed on them for centuries untold.

James does not want to follow that trail. Too many children have gone down just such a dark path and never returned. Yet he can feel the draw of it. He can feel the cold in his chest, and he knows that as long as Elffingern possesses his severed finger, the wraith will sup at it — at his soul — to keep itself alive. That the ice will continue to creep into his limbs until he will no longer know what warmth feels like, and he grows cold, pale and stiff, like William had.

But it will not be enough. Elffingern is too old, too burdened with the weights of so many souls for the taste of just one to revive it. It will cower and sap James' life, until they both perish in the blinding chill.

All this James can feel in the clatter of dry bone between his fingers. He can feel it in the lure of warm blood that tempts him across the snow, into the dark between the trees. Perhaps he can dare it. Perhaps he can best the wounded beast and win back his prized finger, the link to his essence, and not live out his days in fear.

But James does not follow the trail of blood — his blood — into the darkness. The thing he faces is ancient and has survived here, in the dark and the cold, by guile and cunning and ruthlessness for so long that even time has forgotten it exists. With difficulty, he loops together the broken strands and drapes them over his neck.

'A trade!' he shouts to the wind, and the trees, and the terror that eats at his bones. 'Mine for yours. I will bring you another soul, and in return, you will release mine. Do this, and I will give all of these back.' He shakes the bones around his neck with his good hand, feeling the cold burrowing into his skin. Already the bones are sinking into him, under his skin, searching for warmth. 'Do we have a deal?'

The wind howls, and the blizzard collapses upon him.

Vierzehn (14)

Mary's hands shook as she set the tenth sheet down.

Stories, just stories.

Her boy's narratives, weaving a disjointed tale fit only for nightmare, couldn't be true. They couldn't possibly reflect anything real, much less what James had seen in the war. They were stories, nothing more. To believe otherwise was too harrowing to contemplate.

Nonetheless, she found herself rising, walking to the door, pushing aside the curtain and looking across the long, dark space that separated the sanctuary of her home from the ink-stained cavern where the press machinery slumbered. The press, with its spinning wheels and grinding teeth and slamming plates, shadowed by the watching pines. And was that a figure, a shambling shade among the shadows, stumbling toward the press door?

Mary was through the door and crossing the empty lot before she had time to consider the danger. She clasped one of the rifles in her hands, though whether it was loaded or if she even knew how to use it were moot points. With any luck, the mere sight of a gun would be enough to frighten any intruder away.

Eric wasn't some trading piece in a deal between the demon and the damned. Eric would not be sacrificed to resurrect a dead ghost, in this young land where there should have been so many dreams, so few nightmares.

Mary heard the terrified cry before she pushed through the door. In the dim pools of illumination cast by two gas lamps, the scene resolved itself in awful, gruesome clarity.

James, leaning over the manual press, one gloved hand wrapped around the plate lever, one gripping Eric's wrist as the boy struggled to get his fingers out from under the machine. Between James and Mary, there moved a hunched figure, bone-thin, limping forward one agonised step at a time, its hands outstretched. On one of these hands, a bloody stump where an eleventh digit ought to have been. In the other, a bleeding finger, pale as snow.

Mary didn't know how she found the courage to move, except that her son — her only son, all that was left of her William — was in danger. She rushed forward, swinging the rifle, slamming the intruder sideways into the bulking mass of the press. The ring of metal on metal was drowned out by the roar of discharging gunpowder.

Mary would never learn why James had hung a loaded gun

over her door. She would never be able to ask him.

The bullet ricocheted off the machinery and slammed into James' ribs, punching through his chest. Shards of red ice scattered and shattered across the dark floor, along with dozens of tiny broken bones.

'Nein,' croaked the demon as it sank to the floor, withering, hands still grasping for Eric. 'Meine...'

'Not yours. Mine.'

Mary brought the rifle butt down with a wet crack, like frozen branches snapping under the weight of too much snow, in a land far away, where fairy tales grew dark claws and hunted in the wake of other men's wars.

The brittle red chunks that had been James' frozen heart began to melt across the concrete, while the finger bones of untold dead mean broke apart and crumbled into dust.

Stepping over Elffingern's still form, Mary pulled Eric close to her, holding him tight, like she would never let war or nightmare take him away from her again. Eric pulled himself closer to his mother, shivering, and ever so gently, rubbed his fingers against hers.

But she doubted she could keep the nightmares away, not for long. Men had ways of making their own horrors, and of bringing them up out of the darkness and into the light. Sometimes, all you needed was the frozen remains of a heart, stripped of everything it had ever loved and laid out to die in the snow. They said that this war, the Great War, could never be repeated, that it would decide, once and for all, the shape of the world. Mary prayed that was true, for if there was to be another, they would surely take her son from her, and she was sure that was a nightmare she could never wake from.

'No more stories,' she whispered to Eric, and he nodded, and wrapped his cold fingers tight around hers.

Author Biographies

Rue Karney is a horror writer and amateur neuroscientist with a love of the bizarre and gruesome. She has worked as an artists' model, barmaid, and frozen food packer, but (apart from writing horror) her most interesting job has been cleaning toilets in a pub in the middle of the desert. When not creating malicious characters and evil scenarios, Rue enjoys learning French and reading about psychopaths. Her work has also appeared in the Hic Dragones anthology, *Hauntings*.

Jason Nahrung grew up on a Queensland cattle property and now lives in Ballarat with his wife, the author, Kirstyn McDermott. He works as an editor and journalist to support his travel addiction. His fiction is invariably darkly themed, perhaps reflecting his passion for classic B-grade horror films and '80s goth rock. His most recent long fiction title is the gothic tale, *Salvage* (Twelfth Planet Press), and the outback vampire duology, *Blood and Dust* and *The Big Smoke* (Clan Destine Press). 'Triage', written specifically for an anthology of the EnVision writers' workshop, marks an early outing for a character from *The Big Smoke* who has, like that novel, gone through a few changes of his own. Jason lurks online at www.jasonnahrung.com

Marty Young is a Bram Stoker nominated and Australian Shadows Award winning editor, fiction and non-fiction writer, and sometimes ghost hunter. He was the founding president of the Australian Horror Writers Association from 2005-2010, and one of the creative minds behind the internationally acclaimed Midnight Echo magazine, for which he also served as executive editor until mid-2013. His website is www.martyyoung.com

Natalie Satakovski is a former English teacher who has turned to copywriting to support her fiction habit. Her work has appeared in AntipodeanSF and Infernal Ink Magazine. She loves reading all things creepy, from southern gothic to the new weird. Tweet things for her to retweet @Satalie

Stuart Olver lives in Brisbane with his wife and two sons. He is the author of the award-winning coffee table book, *The Scenic Rim*, and would spend all his time exploring and photographing mountains if he could. In 2014, he won the AHWA Flash Fiction competition with his story, 'What Came Through'.

J. Ashley Smith is a British-Australian writer of dark fiction and other materials, some of which can be found at www.jashleysmith.com. He is the 2015 winner of the AHWA Short Story competition for his tale, 'On the Line'. He lives in the Blue Mountains of New South Wales (where there are many leeches), tormenting himself with nightmares while his wife and two sons sleep.

Cameron Trost is a writer of strange, mysterious, and creepy tales about people just like you. His short stories have been published in dozens of magazines and anthologies, including Midnight Echo, Morpheus Tales, and Crowded Quarantine's *Of Devils and Deviants*. His collection, *Hoffman's Creeper and Other Disturbing Tales*, is available from Black Beacon Books. He is the vice-president and Queensland community leader of the Australian Horror Writers' Association, and a member of the Queensland Writers' Centre. Rainforests, thunderstorms, whisky, and chess are a few of his favourite things. Visit him at www.trostlibrary.blogspot.com

Joanne Anderton writes speculative fiction with anime and manga influences. She sprinkles a little science fiction to spice up her fantasy, and thinks a touch of horror adds flavour to everything. Her novels, *Debris*, *Suited*, and *Guardian*, have been published by Angry Robot Books and Fablecroft Publishing. Her short story collection, *The Bone Chime Song and Other Stories* won the Aurealis Award for best collection, and the Australian Shadows Award for best collected work. Visit her online at www.joanneanderton.com

Mark McAuliffe lives in Brisbane. Since the 1990s, he has had stories and poetry appear in several small press publications, including Skinned alive, E.O.D. and Daarke Worlde. More recently, he has been published in the ezines, Eclecticism, and AntipodeanSF, as well as the anthologies, *An Eclectic Slice of Life* (Dark Prints Press), and *Til Death Do Us Part* (Burnt Offerings Books).

Mark Smith-Briggs is the president of the Australian Horror Writers' Association. His short fiction has appeared in magazines and anthologies in Australia, the US, and Canada, while his non-fiction and review work in the genre has won a Chronos Award and been nominated for two Ditmars. He lives in Melbourne where he works as an editor with Leader Newspapers. Find him at www.freewebs.com/marksmithbriggs

Kathryn Hore is a Melbourne writer, photographer and occasional librarian. She writes speculative fiction and business non-fiction, with fiction appearing in a variety of anthologies and magazines, including the AHWA's own Midnight Echo, and a novel in the works. She takes photos of weddings and spiders, though not usually at the same time, and has a website she occasionally remembers to update: www.letmedigress.com

Anthony Ferguson has published short stories, flash fiction pieces, and non-fiction articles in Suspect Thoughts, Camp Horror, Lost Souls, Ripples, Horrorscope, MicroHorror, Midnight Echo, and the anthology, *RomComZom*. He wrote the non-fiction book, *The Sex Doll: A History* (McFarland 2010), and edited the short story collection, *Devil Dolls and Duplicates in Australian Horror* (Equilibrium 2011). He was awarded second prize in the AHWA/Melbourne Zombie Convention 2013 Short Story Competition, and received an honourable mention in the AHWA 2014 Flash Fiction Competition. He blogs at www.apferguson.com

Steve Cameron is a Scottish/Australian writer who currently resides in the eastern suburbs of Melbourne, Australia. When not writing, he teaches English at a local secondary college. Steve maintains a website at www.stevecameron.com.au

Dan Rabarts is the winner of New Zealand's Sir Julius Vogel Award for Best New Talent, 2013. His short stories have appeared in Beneath Ceaseless Skies, ASIM, and Midnight Echo, and in the anthologies *Bloodstones*, *Regeneration*, and *The Mammoth Book of Dieselpunk*, among many others. The horror flash fiction anthology, *Baby Teeth: Bite-sized Tales of Terror*, which he co-edited with Lee Murray, won the SJV for Best Collected Work, and the Australian Shadows Award for Best Edited Work. Find out more at www.dan.rabarts.com

Australian Horror Writers' Association

www.australianhorror.com

Made in the USA
Lexington, KY
27 February 2017